I0700524

Fuckboy Problems

This book is dedicated to my beloved Willow and the women who are still learning about life and all of the things that it has to offer.

|1|
ENTER THE FUCKBOY

In my short but informative thirty-three years of living my life in this insane world, I have met many people. There are people that I met in the past who made me realize that there was more to life than I ever could have imagined as a child. They were people who I wanted to keep in my life for the long run. The kind that make you think about life beyond the scope of believing that there is no such thing as true love and push you to be the best you that you can be.

They made me realize there is much more to life than just going out and struggling to make ends meet. These are ones that you should surround yourself with and keep if possible. Whenever I met people like this, I never wanted to see them go; but there is this crazy thing about life, most times, you often don't control who comes and goes. Sometimes, people you fight so hard to keep in your life because of how peaceful they make you feel end up being the first to leave, although that's a story for another day.

Just as I met people who added a lot of meaning to my life, I also met people who came into my life only to wreck the ship I had been struggling so hard to sail on. These are the ones who take more than they ever add and would hang around like the plague even when I wanted nothing more than to be as far away from them as possible. Among these people is this special group of people that we have so affectionately coined as fuckboys and they will destroy your life if given the opportunity. Trust me I know. Dating is damn near impossible in this generation thanks to a multitude of different things, but the one thing that sticks out the most that ruins it is them.

Now J, what the hell is a fuckboy some of you may ask? And luckily, most of us know exactly the type that I am referring to, but for the ones who do not, the Urban Dictionary/Word Hippo defines a "fuckboy" as a young man (or old one) of poor judgment or taste, especially one who is perceived as cowardly or who tries too hard to be cool. We meet many of them in our lives for different reasons like to gain experience or turn to new chapters, but they are the absolute worst to encounter. Women tend to be given a sixth sense at birth that alerts us when things are array but we will ignore every ounce of our common sense once we run into the right one or the wrong one rather.

There is an interesting thing about our lives as individuals, which includes the plans that we make for ourselves growing up. When we are young, everyone begins drawing out these meticulous plans. We normally have it set in our minds at an early age that we want the best for ourselves. As children, we grow up dreaming of becoming things that are displayed by society as prestigious such as a doctor, lawyer, scientist, etc. when in reality, these occupations are over-glorified and cost thousands of dollars in debt to achieve, and let's just face the facts not everyone is cut out to be a doctor. I know quite a few people that, I know for a fact, I would not want to be the surgeon I see waking up from anesthesia and I know that ya'll do too. The plans that we begin to put in place are important because of how much we want everything to turn out exactly how we anticipated they would but when it is all said and done, we end up finding out that things don't always work out like we thought they were going to. Sometimes even the smallest, insignificant thing comes up and changes everything.

Most women at a young age ingrained in our brain that we never want to have anything to do with a man that would look down on us or that we don't ever want to be with a man that would disrespect us and then attempt to do everything in our power to stand our ground and make sure that we don't end up going against the standards we set, and yet we end up still falling for a fuckboy. We bend the rules and break our own hearts and codes for gremlins that do not deserve a second glance. They're like bugs. One day you're relaxing minding your own business and one suddenly appears, begging for attention, and being annoying. We have all been there and done that or will at some point in our lifetime.

Now according to Dictionary.com, a fuckboy is that guy who doesn't respect women but relies on them heavily for gratification, financial reasons, or any other type of gain that you can think of. He is usually self-absorbed, doesn't care about other people's time, and fucks with others' emotions just for the hell of it. The best description for a fuckboy is that guy that would go to any length and do everything that might seem right to them, and maybe even right in your eyes, just to get what they want.

My first question to you is, are fuckboys born or made? In a world full of throat babies and bust down thotianas what molds a man to define how he will treat women, even the ones who aren't that type? I say for the ones who do treat women badly, this usually, not in every case, stems from mommy issues that roll over into their adult lives, so they feel the need to treat women as objects like what they grew up seeing done to their mothers, sisters, aunts, etc. They grew up in an unfavorable family setting, which ended up making them develop a certain way of thinking.

Although I understand that not all of us grow up in a perfect sitcom or "family matters" environment, it is still no excuse. Someone eventually has to break the generational curse. The statement, "that's just how I am," has become a well-known scapegoat for individuals to use to excuse their learned miscreant behavior. On the other hand, you also have men who grew up well loved and molded, got hurt, and decide to be assholes, just because.

Britney Spears warned us about them in her 2003 song "Toxic." Now I'm not saying a man is the reason for her baldheaded breakdown, but I'm sure it played a part. Women tend to get so caught up in the lies of a womanizer on the premise of love and don't see the red flags until it is too late. My best friend and I always make jokes that we think we might be able to use bleach and turn the flag pink but Nah. These red flags are made of some impenetrable polyester that stays red until the day that they are thrown out in the garbage where they belong. I remember growing up and watching the men in my family run through women and I never knew the danger that I was going to encounter as an adult. To a fuckboy, women are nothing more than play things.

The funny thing is that men love a chase, but if it's too easy, they get uninterested; we could easily compare them to babies with every toy imaginable that you would think a baby should love but instead, they choose to play with simple objects like your keys or pull all of the baby wipes out the container instead then move on to the next thing that they have no business messing with. All they know how to do is put anything they can get their hands on in their mouths, sleep, and shit. At this point, they are viewed as wreckless. These little boys, because they are most certainly not men, tend to be more careless in playing with toys. They make messes and jump and climb all over things but are always excused by the fact that "boys will be boys."

As you probably have noticed already, I do not recommend falling for a fuckboy because they will screw you over every chance they get. Once a fuckboy, always a fuckboy.

This word may sound new to some people, but the truth is that they have been around for quite some time. Back in the day, women kept quiet and weren't allowed to freely express what they wanted. Well, let me tell you, it is 2022 and we are not our ancestors baby. Betty Jean that used to wash and fold clothes sun up to sun down and have dinner ready, is gone. We were known to be malleable and accommodating, but now we have Megan Thee Stallion, Cardi B, and various women that are the representation young women are seeing and striving to be like more and more because it seems like what men want these days.

Yet, they complain about these very same women on social media all the time. And say that they want a "good" woman knowing good and damn well that they are lusting after the half-naked ones and liking all of their pictures. Social media has become such a huge moral dilemma for men and women because everyone has their opinions on certain situations, but unlike before the internet, now everyone can make their opinion known.

I know ya'll didn't ask for my two cents, but you're reading this so, in my opinion being in a relationship is all about making efforts. Most of us as human beings strive to be in a healthy one. For a relationship to survive and become stronger and more suitable, those involved have to keep making efforts to be there for their significant other and not try to replicate what they've seen on TV or Instagram. A good relationship should be such that those involved will usually begin thinking about having a future together.

Normally, when people are in a serious relationship, they develop a strong urge to seek things becoming permanent between them and their significant other. It's in our nature to, of course, start thinking about our future with the person that we fall in love with because if not then what are you even doing? Whenever we think about our future, we will include that person in it, and there will hardly be any plan that doesn't include our man, but if this person is a fuckboy, he, of course, is not thinking about any of that. After establishing a connection or getting hooked on a fuckboy, we sometimes become damaged in ways that cannot be seen.

Being in a relationship with a fuckboy is a whole different ballgame. These niggas, I mean people, can pretend to be angels and impersonate the role of anybody. You can bet your ass that they know how to give an Oscar-worthy performance of being the most romantic person you've ever met just to get to any objective that they've mapped out in their evil little minds before they approach you. Once they have an idea that they did that, their true colors start to come out and you better believe them the first time. This is going to be the exact moment in time that you can see them for who they truly are. In the blink of an eye, you'll wonder where that demon standing there came from and need to grab some holy water.

They may make compromises at first, but once they can quit being conniving and pretending, they'll stop attempting to do that quick. What is the point of being in a relationship with someone who isn't willing to compromise? One of the top three ways to be someone's peace is something as simple as compromising, which usually entails figuring out their love language. If someone loses interest in doing that, then you should realize that the only person they really care about is themselves and that they are not worried about you or your happiness.

But back to the matter at hand. Again, men love a chase more than some of us love lace fronts and lash extensions, but from my experience with fuckboys, it doesn't always work like that with them. It doesn't matter how long it takes for them to get at a particular woman. If it took some time to get in a woman's head, it might take them a bit longer to fuck her over, but screwing her over is a thing that they are inevitably planning to do. Their favorite line is, "the last thing that I want to do is hurt you." That may be so, but it's on the list. It's literally on the list as the last thing written in all caps. And if the chase is too easy for them, they will most likely start showing who they are quicker.

Fuckboys only know how to eat and satisfy their own inhibitions. They are shallow assholes. A shallow person is a person that doesn't think deeply about the action which they intend to take. Isaac Newton said in his third law of motion that "for every action, there is an equal and opposite reaction." What this means is that for every action we take, there is, in any event, a reaction that is near. Whatever effort we make, whether in a positive or negative direction, something always ends up deriving from it, and whatever ends up happening will solely depend on you as a person. Whatever you reap, you sow, as the old folks used to say. I don't know if ya'll believe in karma but I do. The only reason some people go about doing what they do to other people is because they don't sit down and think about how the hell they would feel if the shoe was on the other foot and some don't care.

We know that everywhere in the world that there are people who commit crimes; some go unnoticed while others are so obvious that they can't be hidden irrespective of how much those that carried them out tried to hide them. Let's look at murder, for example; some of the reasons people are killed here in the U.S is senseless, but it doesn't stop people from doing it. Do the people who take someone else's life for the dumbest reason think about the consequences of their actions? Do they consider the pain of what they did will cause? Some do and some don't. Same as a fuckboy. When someone is murdered, the main people who have to carry the burden are their loved ones, and they are the ones that are going to mourn for a long time after the fact. Family members are the ones that are going to miss this person, and they are the ones that will have to endure the pain associated with their absence.

A lot of us have experienced the immense agony caused by things like this, but not everyone has had this happen to them. With that being the case, do you think that they think about it? Or take serial killers, for instance; they kill multiple people and sleep peacefully with their fans on high until they get caught and locked up. Same goes for fuckboys; these are the same ones who fuck over good people and then want to cry "put some money on my books," or "free my ninja," knowing good and well that they fucked up. One of the signature moves of a fuckboy is to reach out to a woman they friend-zoned after they are done playing mind games and their dick is dried up trying to come back and disturb her peace again.

Most people, doing either right or wrong, have reasons why they believe they are doing what they are supposed to. Whether it's reasonable or not, the truth of the matter is that the main difference between someone doing good and someone doing bad is the limitation. For those that are shallow-minded, their actions come from their reflexes. They come from a dark place that has already been instilled in them. It comes from something in them, that is, them. Like when people say things bluntly and pretend like what they said is coming from a good place, but you already know how they really feel based on the shit that they dared to let come out of their mouth. Please, that could be a good thing for someone who needs to hear the truth or devastating to someone with a fragile mental well-being but they don't think about that part.

I am convinced that fuckboys do know when they do people wrong. They always have it somewhere in the back of their minds before they decide to do it, but at that point, they simply want to and say fuck how it turns out. This is because if they were not shallow-minded individuals, they wouldn't have even given a second thought about doing it in the first place. People with hearts empathize beforehand. When you put yourself in someone else's shoes, you realize that your actions could possibly be the most damaging thing to that person's mind, body, or soul even.

I'm not saying that a fuckboy can't have a heart. Although, it seems like these soulless creatures don't. Perhaps they are not trying to be vindictive over something terrible that happened to them in the past, but because they have built up this impenetrable wall they think that they should never let the same thing that they do to other people get done to them. This makes them known for exhibiting heartless behavior and end up doing childish things just for approval. We all know at least one petty male individual who does anything for likes just to claim that they're the G.O.A.T in front of their nothing-ass friends.

If not, I can guarantee that you know someone who is always preaching about what's right or wrong, like Pastor Woodbine. The ones who always criticize things or people and tell everyone that cares to listen that whatever it is isn't right, but years later we come to find out that they are doing the same damn thing they said they'd NEVER do? Like us saying we would not date an asshole but still wind up in an entanglement with one.

Have you ever asked yourself, why do people treat people who have had the same thing done to them the same way and they know that it hurts? People did the same thing to them and although they felt that shit in their chest, they still choose to do it to someone else and watch as their life becomes a living hell for their enjoyment. There are a lot of TV shows that target addiction and the main reason why the character of interest on the show ends up with an addiction is because of things done to them in the past, that they refuse to let go of, and chose to cope negatively because of it.

Their actions are a result of what they have experienced in the past and it unfailingly boils down to the motive for why they are that way. A fuckboy, most times, has just one motive, which is to give themselves what they want, which can include sex or whatever strokes their ego. Whenever a fuckboy does anything, it doesn't matter what it is. There's always a catch.

If you find yourself getting attached to a fuckboy, thinking of him all day, getting butterflies, and wondering if you may have a future together, you better believe that they are not thinking about anything close to identical. So many women out here may not look like it but have been damaged in several ways due to relationships that they have gotten suckered into. A closer view can reveal that these are mainly women involved with them.

It doesn't matter the degree of sacrifice which you have made for them in the past, and it also doesn't matter the degree of sacrifice that you may currently be making for a fuckboy, once it comes to the point when they are expected to make a sacrifice, be prepared because they will consistently choose themselves over you. I am not advocating for people to go around doing things to please others and end up not being happy themselves, but we all know how the song by Lauryn Hill goes. When it hurts so bad, why does it feel so good? When a woman chooses to make sacrifices for the one she loves and continues to put her heart on the line, doesn't she deserve just a little gratitude in return? We all do.

Sometimes, when we talk about making sacrifices, some people view it as something far-fetched. Call it instinct, like a tiger who needs to eat and doesn't care whether its prey is small and weak or big and strong; this is a typical description of a fuckboy. I have seen it a million times; a man with multiple women who he is romantically involved with makes all of them believe that he cares about them faster than Amazon can deliver a package, hell maybe even that he loves them but doesn't. They think that they are the only ones so they commit and do all they can to make everything work but end up getting destroyed in the process. He thinks it's cool until a woman ends up going Jazmine Sullivan on his ass.

Some people build up particular defenses or bad habits to protect themselves, and the person that suffers most becomes the next good guy that finds his way into their life. Hence good men get hit with the friend zone. Oh, the dreaded friend zone. It is a real place and men and women of all types sometimes end up there. It's a proven fact that most women indeed tend to gravitate towards assholes when looking for a relationship. Why? Don't ask me. Crazy? Maybe. But I do the same thing and whew, let me tell you, it usually never ends up pleasantly.

As for him, he just sees them as his prey like the others. Most of us don't even know when a man has someone else until it is too late because there is always this false sense of safety they portray that tells us that we should believe him. The biggest enemy of man is man himself. People who hurt people that love them are the most toxic people ever. Love is one of the highest gifts that one can give to another. Imagine the beautiful feeling that comes to your mind when you love freely, and your love is really coming from the bottom of your heart without it being coerced or influenced.

There is nothing like the feeling that comes with knowing that you love someone and that person loves you back. Love brings together bonds that even blood can't break. This is what only love can do, and yet, this same love that gets given to some may be given to a person that doesn't want the same and takes advantage of it. Unrequited love. This is a common trend among fuckboys.

This might sound crazy, but something ironic that I have found out is that you can approach people with the very best intentions in your heart, but they may approach you with the worst of their own. So, the best way to combat that is to be prepared, right? In this book, if you choose to keep reading, I will help you recognize the types of fuckboys and how to avoid them. The benchmark story of men and women is of Adam and Eve or some story with the plight of a damsel in distress falling prey to something or someone she had no business dealing with to begin with. I think it's time that we change that narrative.

|2|
CHARACTERISTICS

Ok, so now that we have a good idea of what a fuckboy is, we can learn to identify their characteristics. We have talked about them and it is no longer news to say that fuckboys are destructive fiends when they find their way into anyone's life.

Nothing can equate to the enormous amount of headaches that fuckboys will undoubtedly bring to the lives of the women that they snake their way into. So many lives were and will be destroyed because of them. So many dreams shattered, and so many smiles turned into wrinkles. The characteristics that they possess can be easily misinterpreted by the untrained eye, but I'm here to help because ain't nobody got time for that.

1. They are mostly subtle. Or should I say they appear very faint to their unsuspecting victims? They give you that first impression that they would be the kind of guys that would never hurt a fly. They give you that feeling that once you are with them, you wouldn't have a single care in the world and that you're going to love it there. This is one of their many manipulation tactics.

Because of their nature, they can make anything seem true. For instance, imagine being out in public and a random woman approached you with some drama or some random chick DM'ed you and told you that they were sleeping with your man. Are you going to get mad and attempt to drag the bitch without even hearing their full story? You might end up blaming the woman instead of him. Why? Because they appear to be innocent. After a woman has been involved with different types and none of them seem to work out, seeing this sweet, appealing face with puppy dog eyes might seem like a breath of the freshest air you can imagine. Don't fall for it. This is the impression that they are trying to give anyone at first glance of him, but it is rarely the case.

Soon after or later you will see that this fool who you thought would give you the peace you are looking for turns out to be the entire opposite of what you thought he was. Then you realize that looks can be one of the biggest elements of deceiving someone. At this point, you, in all likelihood, already love him. He will continue to wreak havoc until the relationship gets brought to an end eventually. While some people with a subtle appearance might give you that warm, fuzzy feeling of being genuine and honest, always have it in the back of your mind that most fuckboys have that type of appearance. Most of them have female tendencies, which is why they know exactly how to charm women.

2. They are, in most cases, very well endowed: most fuckboys are good-looking. They are good-looking, and they know it. They know this is one of the weaknesses that most of us have and they can position it as a trap for us. It is more common that a good-looking guy is going to try to play you. When you look at them closely, you find out that they don't have much to offer other than their good looks and can't tell their head from their ass. I may catch some backlash or scrutiny for this or this entire book, but most of them have nose rings. It's all out in the open now. I don't know why but there is something about a man with a nose ring that screams fuckboy.

They are the ones that are proud to show off in front of other women, like wearing grey sweatpants with a print, and will get the biggest head while accepting compliments about it. They take forever to get ready to go out, probably staring in the mirror admiring themselves or at the barbershop because they worship their image more than anything and spend more on beauty products than women. It is good to look good, but sweet baby Jesus there is a limit. I wouldn't talk bad about anybody that wants to look good, we all do, but we know one person who makes trying to look good sickening and just does too much.

In their fun-size, little brains people of this caliber see themselves as idols that should be adored because they believe they look better than everyone around them. Getting a compliment from anyone means that they are doing the job right, so they will do any and everything they can to stay gainfully employed. Even when someone is not saying anything to them at all, just getting those "how you doin?" looks or being asked what kind of cologne they are wearing literally makes their heads bigger. People of this nature are the staple of what being a fuckboy entails.

Another way that we may look at being endowed is when we consider the size of their dick. While some people may have a small one, others happen to be average some others are working with monsters and are blessed. Some prefer average sizes and that's their business, but the majority end up choosing men for the opposite reason. Some fuckboys have big dicks and don't know how to use it. How or why? I have no clue, but most that do have a big dick know how to use them well because they have had plenty of practice.

They know that you know that they know how to use it. They know that once you get some, you get dickmatized. Yes dickmatized, it's a real word; look it up, and it becomes a plus for them because now they can most definitely use it against you. Their dick becomes a selling point for them; they start acting as if the whole world revolves around it. A male friend of mine calls his "the act right" but constantly has women busting his windows and slashing three of his tires instead of all of them.

The ones who aren't as blessed as others in the dick department know how to use their mouth baby. They have learned how to eat a pudding cup without a spoon. If you know, you know. Get into a disagreement with one and watch how they eat you like groceries to try and make up. This brings me to my next point.

3. They are always good with conversation and can use their mouth in more ways than one. Do you ever wondered why it is always easy for them to convince you to agree with some of the things they say even if you totally disagree? It's because they are good at asking and good at making conversation, especially men with shaved heads. They know exactly how to tell us those smooth, bald-headed lies to rope our asses right on in.

Fuckboys are good with their mouth in a number of ways. One of the things that attract a woman to a man is how good he is with communication. It is easier for a woman to fall for a man who is good at initiating and keeping a conversation than it is for her to fall for someone who isn't.

They are so good at talking that when they do something that looks suspicious and you try to point it out or argue it's child play how easily the fuckers can turn your whole mood or day around with just one lie. They have the ability to paint a lie so good that it becomes almost impossible to differentiate the truth from the lie. I've met my share of pathological liars. If you have one hitting on you, trying too hard to impress you, and everything he says seems too perfect, watch him. When everything he says seems to be too organized or effortless and he can easily win you over, I repeat, WATCH THAT MAN; this is a fuckboy. If you happen to invite a "sweet talker" into your life, it will end up being lie after lie. Trusting them is like trusting someone who says their dog doesn't bite when it's clearly a ravenous pit bull.

One thing you must know is that most fuckboys are really good at hitting on women and talking a woman out of her draws, as they say. This is because they have had several instances where they talked to so many girls and ended up winning their hearts with quick lies, so they have had years of practice. Not every smooth talker is a fuckboy, but you have to watch out for this because they are the main ones.

4. In some cases, they may have a little money, but there are a lot of fuckboys that are broke. These are the ones who come into your life begging and are damn near homeless. They'll end up leaching on to you with their well-thought-out lies in an attempt to turn you into their main source of finances or to find somewhere to

stay. We call these hobosexuals. They love telling a good sob story or turning on the waterworks to get you to trust them. I have learned that if someone's family doesn't fool with them, there is a reason and you apparently shouldn't either.

There are many fuckboys out there that try to put on like they are rich. The first notable sign of a fuck boy is the type of car that they drive. If he has a Challenger, Charger, or Mustang, you guessed it. They might as well go ahead and have the title of "unsavory gentleman" plastered to their forehead. In their testosterone-filled world, having a fast car may be the only thing, they have to make up for other areas that they are lacking in. Or they may stay in name brand and a fresh fit, but don't even have a car.

Some do have money and will surely throw it in your face. They'll come at you looking extra flashy and nice with their clean cars and chains, nice Gucci belts, and Balenciaga shoes so that you think they are ready to spend it all on you. Chances are they are willing to drop a bag on you because they know that it can get them whoever or whatever they want, no questions asked. Their wealth is the only thing that they can bring to the table. They are people who, whenever an issue arises, can't pass up the opportunity in an argument to remind you that they are the ones funding you. That Burkin bag may be nice but might not be worth the frustration.

Because they are spending money or providing for you, they literally see themselves as your owner. One thing for certain is that they will have a sense of entitlement. They feel like they are inclined to have you, and your time and that they own every bit of you because they are materialistic. They feel like whenever they ask for something from you, you have no right to give an excuse why you can't see or do things their way. Most of them are used to gold diggers who have no problem obliging their ridiculous demands, so they expect it. And honey please, this is ain't that.

5. Another very well-known quality of a fuckboy is that they are proud. This is always one thing that will easily give them away. Most men would rather die than admit that they are broke or dead ass wrong. Another red flag. At least it helps in distinguishing between rich men that are into you for real and rich men that are fuckboys. The fuckboys that fall into this category won't hesitate to tell you exactly how much their jewelry or car costs, they'll tell you how much the shoes on their feet cost,

and they might even let you know how expensive their house is (if they have even had one), and about how they only fly first class, in most cases, we don't even care. The women who care are usually not the type they go after. Some women enjoy this type of relationship and will do whatever it takes to keep getting that bag. To each its own.

There are a lot of other characteristics of fuckboys. Another thing about them is that they enjoy how simple it is for them to attract the opposite sex and we fall for it every single time. They have this aura about them that keeps us intrigued and are hard to resist. If you do end up resisting, maybe it was because you have heard what they are about.

On another spectrum, female celebrities we know and love end up victims of fuckboys as well. They can't go to all of the places they want to without being hassled, so they end up dating a rapper and I hate to step on some toes, but fuckboys are the byproducts of the music industry. They bask in their lifestyles in awe and try so bad to be that dude or as close to the carbon copy image as possible. One big truth about the life of a celebrity is that they sometimes live lonely lives and it's not as glamorous as they make it seem. Take the

Kardashians, for example; we all know that they struggle in the relationship department.

This originates from the relationships that we have with our families. Trauma bonding is a common denominator when it comes to the type of men we choose. And by trauma bonding, I mean that something from the past has hindered us from realizing our self-worth and true potential. While growing up, I was around a lot of men and they all say that it is not difficult to make a woman fall for them. On any given day, you can often see a group of men having a casual conversation, and I bet you may hear one of them say, "man, just tell her this. She will believe you." It is effortless for some of them to convince a woman with just his words alone.

In other words, women fall easily for whatever a man tells her, and it is most likely words from a man they happen to love. A lot of fuckboys already know this, and they use it as leverage to unleash their paws on women whom they scoped out and already know are going to go for it. These men believe that the words that come out of their mouths alone are the sole reason they can control and manipulate a woman into whatever they want her to do or be. I would say this is true because over the years, it has been a growing trend and a lot of fuckboys use it as the basis for their fucked up actions towards women.

It doesn't matter, whatever they do, and it doesn't matter how horrible they treat the women in their life. Whenever you feel wronged, they will just say a few words to get you back to the mental space where they want you to be, and if it becomes difficult with words, they will figure out an alternative. We tend to get caught up in lies and don't see the signs until it is too late. We say that we will never put up with a cheater and it is the same story with just about anyone that you meet in the world. One of the biggest reasons we have such a high divorce rate is because one party was dishonest. Make it make sense? This makes me not even want to get married and other people feel the same.

Domestic violence is also a serious matter that is often overlooked behavior exhibited by fuckboys, and it has led to the deaths of many. Sometimes it is hard to see when you love that person. For someone to die from domestic violence doesn't mean that person was the weak one among the two. Domestic violence is very common in many marriages; it's just that so many people tend to be quiet about it. Even women can initiate domestic violence against their partner; we have seen it happen recently between a well-known rapper and his girl. How embarrassing.

In either situation, the victim feels like they are the one to blame. Some people fight battles that we have no clue about. We rarely hear about this until it is too late and then say well, she/he was dumb for staying. But in an actual sense, it rarely becomes the reason for breakups. Especially in marriage because that is what the victim has grown accustomed to and thinks it is what love is despite it being hammered into our brains at a young age that it is not.

Most men find it difficult for whatever reason to be faithful to just one woman. For some reason, instead of leaving a person alone, they will find ways to argue to have an excuse to do as they please. I feel like this is childish as hell. They always blame it on one thing or another, but that's the fact of what our everyday life is gradually turning into, something almost all of us vowed never to do, which is accepting cheating.

Most people who cheat do the most. They will find any way to say "it wasn't me," like the infamous song by Shaggy or "you're trippin." When a woman trusts a man, she trusts him wholeheartedly because he hasn't given her a reason not to. Even though they have a gut feeling, they will put up with it for an extended period of time for various reasons. Some people will even have friends that keep telling them that their man is cheating on them, but they never believe it. This could be due to a fear factor that was established by their partner, the promise of gifts and extra affection once the dirt is done, or just because they don't want to be alone.

This is a popular subject displayed on TV shows like P-Valley and it happens more often than we think in real life. Some people might even fall out with their friend who keeps telling them that their man has been cheating on them and only has their best interest at heart. This continues until they end up seeing the truth in all the lies that this man who claimed to love them had been saying to them. At this point, relationships between friends and family members become tarnished beyond repair. There's a type of moral code between friends, but love can break those boundaries. So do you keep your mouth shut and watch your friend keep getting hurt or speak up?

She probably knows already sis and just keeps quiet. No one wants to be embarrassed. She wasn't putting up with all those lies because she knew he was cheating and decided to turn a blind eye to it. She may be cheating too or he was simply deceiving her all along, and because she loves him, she became so vulnerable that she let her guard down. He knew it and then took advantage of the opportunity and continued lying to her. This is what a fuckboy does.

Most women who get lied to countless times by the man that they love are almost never complete fools like everyone thinks. They become numb. When you meet them, you might see them as tough individuals that rarely let anything get to them. They appear to be some of the smartest people in their field and far from slow. I can't say the same about all. We all have had a work bestie who was or is the absolute best at their job in our eyes, very observant, detail-oriented, and cautious about everything they do, nothing ever gets past them; but in the break room, they tell you things about their man going upside their head and you're like girl why do you stay?

I can't help but wonder how Yvette from Baby Boy didn't know that Jody was sneaking around with

Pandora before picking her up from work. Psst. She knew but chose to ignore it when that thang started thangin. But once again, love comes into play and Jody had her dickmatized; that was it. And there's that word again. Being dickmatized will have all of your common sense turn Ray Charles or Love Jones. This is why he was able to continue lying to them, and they continued believing him without finding out that he was lying. They became victims of the lies over an extended period without knowing they were being victimized.

One crazy thing about lies is that at some point, they blow up in whoever is telling them's face. Pathological liars always require more lies to cover up the lies they are lying about. It gets deep sometimes, but a mistake will be made and I can guarantee there will not be a pretty outcome. My thing is, why not just tell the truth? Because that would expose all that they have been doing and mess up their "good thing," and end up making them have to dust that bike off.

Every woman has detective skills, some more than others. They become activated when we start suspecting the man that our man is doing something wrong. Like why does that same girl keep kekeke-ing at everything and hearting everything that he posts?

Now it's time to get that one friend involved who can find out more than the FBI. The problem is he is going to deny, deny, deny no matter what.

Normally, a woman who starts dating someone new begins by scoping his page, more than when they have been dating for a while. They continue to check until they gradually fall off their game after becoming comfortable with him. When you get a new product, it interests you so much that you dedicate most of your time to learning how it works and forget about the other old shit that you already had before; but with time, when everything settles, you stop paying attention because the new thing turns into an old one like the others and you think that you know it like the back of your hand. This is a common mistake that most of us make when dealing with a fuckboy.

If the man is a fuckboy, he will try to hide as much of his real self as he can and knows once you get comfortable, you ain't checking his pages like you used to. He can post a few pictures of ya'll together every now and then to pacify you and still be in the next chick's inbox. He can tell you that whoever is a family member of his and his family will lie for him. His family is not yours. This is rule number one.

It happens the same way with most fuckboys. At the beginning of the relationship, even when women activate our detective instincts, we may end up not finding anything because he swept all of his dirt under the rug. He might be serious about you at the time or might have lost interest in his fuck buddies for the moment, but after a while, they gradually go back to their old ways. At this point, your guard is down, and even though he cheated on his last girl, he would never do you like that other girl because you're better than her, right? WRONG!

This could be going on for a long period; days, weeks, months and you don't even know that the man that you are with, cook for, sleep with, laugh with, even defend from your friends and family, has been cheating repeatedly when you weren't looking until that one thing makes you go "hmm." That's when those "Taken" skills come out full swing. Remember the girl he said was just his homegirl and they just smoke together or the lady he works with starts giving you dirty looks?

Yeah, there's probably something going on there and you might want to look at her sideways back when you get that feeling; chances are that you are no doubt right. I'm definitely not the type to go through phones or tell anyone else to because my grandmother always told me if you go looking for dirt, you are going to get dirty and that hurt will make you unable to eat for days and ugly crying in the car or pillow. No one wants to believe that this could be them until you find the one thing that confirms it.

Some women ask themselves how they could be so dumb for so long and blame themselves for being bamboozled. Unless he was doing it in plain sight, it is not your fault sis. As I said before, no woman in their right mind likes to be cheated on. Nevertheless, we can't look past the fact that we choose the fuckboys. It doesn't mean that it doesn't hurt any less when we find out the truth. Even after ignoring all of the red flags, some women still continue to put up with it. Where do we draw the line?

The women that end up putting up with a man that cheats on them are again either cheating themselves, or they have an issue with their self-esteem. Staying with a cheater is the most detrimental thing that a woman could put herself through because when men cheat, they downgrade. This could be a factor as to why some women lose their self-esteem. There are numerous reasons why some women end up losing their self-confidence, some of them could be a result of deeply seeded family issues or the environment that they grew up in, but one of the most common causes of it is when a woman has been exposed to a fuckboy over an extended period of time.

Most people don't even know what it feels like to be truly loved yet. For all of their lives, the relationships that they have been exposed to have been somewhat exploitive or degrading, the men that wound up being in their lives have been manipulative, these men are abusive in the worst ways ever. Even after the continuous abuse the woman remains with them and they continue dealing with the abuser until they gradually begin losing their self-respect.

A woman doesn't lose her self-esteem in a single day. The journey to losing it is a gradual, tedious process. Sometimes, it doesn't get completed in one single relationship. Some people in their previous relationships were misfortunate enough to encounter a fuckboy. In their present relationship, which is different from the old one, they are still hooked to a fuckboy just a different kind who, though different from the previous one, ends up being just like the rest, if not worse.

For some people, it comes from one single relationship. For others, it comes from several relationships that follow the same bad pattern. Whether it was a single relationship or a series of relationships, the main thing here is that the woman was taken advantage of in some shape, form, or fashion; she was treated badly, made to feel worthless, cheated on, and all these things took a toll over time. Instead of us realizing the power that we have and finding our inner bad bitch we are unable to find the motivation because we have continued working so hard to make something that shouldn't last, even when it is obvious that it should have been over but we're hoping that the person will change overnight but that never happens.

One of the main reasons why some of us remain in a bad relationship for so long is because we are hoping that our partner will change. We have this belief that things will start getting better one day, but another thing is that in the course of waiting for him to change, there is irreversible damage being done to our mental health. Some people find themselves in a relationship that they put their heart and soul into, hoping that it will work out, but in the end, the relationship leaves them broken with a bad taste in their mouths of the opposite sex.

Women get exposed to different unbearable situations that would make others fold; men do as well yet still remain in the tumultuous relationships. The funny thing is that most of the time, these may be people that would never take any shit from anyone, but because they are in love and have grown too weak from their feelings end up doing just that. In fact, they become so weak in making decisions that the person they once were begins to fade forever. When you look at their lives, you discover that every decision they make might be geared more towards pleasing the significant other in their life rather than pleasing themself. At this point there is the realization that they have totally lost their true self. It is an easy thing to do, trust me. And it will make you end up doing things that you said you never would.

I have heard of women who end up apologizing to remain in the life of a man who cheated on them. This is how badly it could affect someone. In Tyler Perry's 2013 film Fighting Temptation, we saw the story unfold of a bored housewife tired of her complacent husband who fell in love with a fuckboy. He treated her horribly and at the end of the story, she was the one who suffered the most at his hands and her ex-husband was happily remarried.

When a relationship is channeled towards ruining your mental health, just leave. Let it burn. I know it's easier said than done. When you find out that the man that claims to love you is a fuckboy that's exactly what you should do. Forget the belief that you can change him. Many lives have been ruined just because they believed that they could change someone who obviously did not want to be changed.

Change is not something that you force onto someone else. As much as change is constant and possible at almost every stage in life, you can't change someone who isn't willing to. For people to drop their bad habits and pick up a new habit that is presumed to be good, they have to be tired of the bad one, they have to hate that bad habit, and they have to really want to do away with it, only then will the struggle for them to change be successful.

You can't change a fuckboy that sees his attitude as something enjoyable. You can't change a fuckboy that knows what he is doing is wrong but is proud of it. These people would rather change you instead and it's easier than you think to lose ourselves. But we must always remember Rule #24.5: "No Crying at the Pynk."

|3|
THE CRAZIES

In my years of vast experience with fuckboys, I have come to realize that there are many different types of fuckboys. You will be amazed once you realize just how many there are living among us in plain sight. There are more than I can tell you about in this book. I'm almost certain that I have not encountered every single type that exists and that I don't intend to. They come in an array of shapes, sizes, ethnicities, backgrounds, etc. Each one, however they choose to present themselves, one thing is for certain is that they always come prepared to cause problems in your life. I'm going to put ya'll up on the game by explaining how to identify the ones that I have met starting with the most common one.

Knowing the types of fuckboys out there will undoubtedly help you figure out how to brace and protect yourself from these vile atrocities that could end up taking you on the roller coaster ride of your life. The first one that we will be discussing is the most infamous, the trademark of fuckboys, the crazy nigga. They always come to steal smiles off the faces of innocent and unsuspecting women. We've all known one. Whether he was ours or one of our friend's problem, nevertheless, they are horrible to deal with. Shit, I think all of them are crazy, but this one, in particular, could, without a doubt, get a check.

Have you ever had a family member that is always going through something? The ones who think everybody around them is crazy, but it's really them? Whenever they are around, there's always a problem, but they pretend that they aren't the root issue or have no idea what the cause is. They always feel like the person that they are dealing with has done something to them, but the whole time they're quite frankly the problem. This is the one who will always talk about how every female they've been with has cheated on them or done something wrong, knowing damn well that they have issues.

These fuckboys will always tell you how they ended up breaking up with someone in the past for a certain reason that had nothing to do with them. "My baby mama/ex was crazy" is their favorite line; they'll also tell you that they don't want you to be like her or that they are talking to you because you aren't; which may seem like a compliment but it isn't. I can guarantee if you find one of these women and inquire about why they broke up, she would say this crazy nigga tried to go upside her head while following her in his car or knocked her between the washer and dryer. The stories told by some of these men always make them look perfect and absolve them from every form of wrongdoing, but there are always two sides to every story. If you get the opportunity to listen to the other side of the same story you will probably regret ever meeting this psychopath.

They complain a lot about how they were omnipotent and how someone ended up taking advantage of them; they complain about how they loved with all their hearts and were disappointed in the end every time with no blood on their hands. Yes, in their own mind, they were the only one that was wronged. They never did anything to warrant getting treated like that. In fact, if there is a possibility for one to be given the title of a saint as a result of how good they are at maintaining a relationship, they believe they should get that title, but all the while they hear voices in their head. They will literally convince themselves that they never do anything unjust. I've worked in psych wards with people who just know they are Jesus and you can not tell them otherwise. Same with fuckboys, not thinking they are Jesus, but you get my drift.

There is always that one dude who undoubtedly uses the phrase 'all women are the same.' Which, of course, we all know is not true. The same goes for men; they are not all the same. The ones who always complains that women are cheaters and never should be trusted by anyone are the ones to be leery of. Whenever you try to talk him out of thinking that, he has made up stories to tell in order to back up his claim knowing that he has been with too many women to count. Sir, they couldn't all have been the problem. At some point and time in life they have to admit that they're the common denominator. Looking at their homeboys, they don't seem to have that issue. If Ike Turner was alive today, I'm sure he would still say that Anna Mae was the problem, but we all know a simple fact, that nigga was CRAZY.

This type of fuckboy thinks that all women want something from them, which we don't because they don't even have anything worth wanting at all except problems. Who wants to deal with a mental patient? This very scenario reminds me of how I've heard a lot of women mention how they want to experience a Joker and Harley Quinn love. The sad thing is that there are so many people out there that think like this. If you only knew the true story behind it, I'm sure that you absolutely would not want that. Yes, I'm sure he loved her and would do anything for her but at what cost?

Some women claim that they want their man to be crazy over them but don't realize how crazy a nigga is until you have wasted so much of your life on them and get so fed up with their crap and have lost yourself in the bullshit and lies. Often, we ask ourselves after dealing with relationships like these, 'how could someone be so cold, callous, and unyielding at the same time? How did I allow myself to fall for this mess? Now I am out chasing this dude, checking his social media, and texting him like I am the crazy one.

The thing about crazy men is that they blame you for their behavior. They'll make excuses like "everyone always leaves me or you're just like them," or "I broke into your house because I love you." Chile, please. This is the same dude that will call our phone private a million times or sit outside your job expecting someone to believe that you did something wrong to him. All of his new girlfriends and family members will end up hating you because this man has made up a thousand and one different stories or twisted the truth to make you seem like the bad guy. When people like this make up stories they seek pity and their stories distort the reality of what is really going on behind closed doors.

A friend of mine was dating a man who was a sociopath. And for those who do not know what a sociopath is, it's another word for batshit crazy. This man literally would do anything in his power to convince her that she was the crazy one, not him. The funny thing is that most people judged from just one side of the story; that side was continuously his. Of course, most of them were his homeboys and when you look at them, they all look like birds of the same feather. So, here go his homies boosting his head up and agreeing that she, in fact, was the problem instead of offering sound advice to him. When they saw her fuck this man up without knowing the whole story due to something that he did, it made his case seem more believable.

He was the kind of guy that never had a female friend that he did not sleep with. I think this is enough to explain the kind of person that he was, whatever the circumstances, in the club every weekend while she stayed home. So, of course, you know that when he got home late, she was wondering why he would put his phone on silent or when they were out in public, she would get the look from his so-called "friends."

They often say that men can't have friends of the opposite sex without sex being involved. This may or may not be true, but the shit that I witnessed thrown her way was definitely not of a friendly manner. His "best friend", let's just call her Ashley, who happened to be a female, ended up homeless because she was living above her means and asked to live with my friend and her man. This was the first red flag in my mind because why would this grown woman not be able to handle her own business, then feel comfortable asking this man to live with him and his girlfriend? I called BS, but Ashley moved into their home and had my friend thinking that he was genuinely being a good friend. I know what you are thinking. She is a whole fool, right? Well, Ashley played the role of a best friend well. She would go shopping with us and act as if nothing was out of the ordinary.

He would degrade her and make her feel stupid for thinking that anything could possibly be going outside of a platonic relationship with this girl. Well, I knew better. Yes ma'am. And after some investigating, she found out they had been sleeping together then and even before him and her got together. And you better believe that Ashley got her ass beat.

The truth is that not all guys are like this, but the ones that get the opportunity to have sex with a friend, 9 times out of ten are going to, even if they have a girlfriend. This is a sad reality that we face and often why women don't want their partners to have female friends. That's kind of unfair when put into perspective, but some women are vindictive and try to do things just for the hell of it. Male friends are less likely to do these types of things because we don't entertain the idea of doing so with them.

I recently saw a video on Facebook of a woman claiming that her friend recently got the infamous BBL done and that she was snatched. From the hips to the waist, this lady described her friend's new body to the tee, then proceeded to say that her friend was ecstatic about coming over for Thanksgiving dinner like she does every year, but she was now unwelcome in her home. The insecurity, of this so-called woman, regarding someone that was supposed to be her friend was disturbing. Instead of supporting her friend and being accepting, she was more worried about her husband being a dog and staring at her friend's new body. The bottom line is that she was jealous or with the wrong man which has caused some insecurity and that's definitely not a friend that I would want in my circle.

I don't think there is anything wrong with a man looking at another woman because it's in their nature to just like we do when we see a nice pair of grey sweatpants. Does that mean that we should not allow our men to have female friends? Of course not. I'm pretty sure that most have thought about wanting to have sex with that one friend of theirs, but when the opportunity comes, they won't act on it; a fuckboy will do it without thinking twice about it.

The guys who have a lot of female friends or are constantly in women's faces, including your friends, are the ones you need to worry about. Attention-seeking whore is a term that I like to use, this can be a male or a female, and they're always all on Snapchat and in the club showing out. Whenever they hang out with a female friend, they expect it to end with getting one thing. In fact, their main plan when they agree to hang out with their female friend or ask their female friend to come over is because they want to get an opportunity to have sex with them. Some men are so obsessed with our body counts being high while theirs is through the roof.

These are classic examples of being a narcissist. This word has gotten thrown around loosely in the past few years and everyone thinks that they have run into one, but when you actually do, you will know for sure that you have. The best word to describe them is 'selfish.' Narcissists are most commonly known for being just that. One thing that they don't mind doing is causing anyone pain because it brings them pleasure. And one crazy thing about dating a narcissist is that despite all of the shit they keep putting you through, somehow, it's still difficult to leave them alone. They fail to see that they are the actual problem.

This is one of the things that a good dick will do to anyone. They might be so damn good in bed that you feel drawn to them even after they continue pushing you to your breaking point. In most cases, something about them keeps making you stay with them. These are the same people who, even though they know they are causing you pain, will still use your pain against you to get exactly what they want, and when you expect them to take pity on you, they twist the knife. Being in love with a narcissist is perhaps like sealing your own fate.

The problem with narcissistic people is not just that they are selfish. They also lack compassion. They are callous in the sense that nothing you have to say really matters to them. It doesn't matter how reasonable what you are trying to say to them is to you, they are right and you can't tell them otherwise. That's where the craziness creeps in; anyone with common sense knows that no one is right one hundred percent of the time. People with this type of sense of entitlement definitely do not care about you or anyone else's feelings.

Can we take a second to talk about soul ties? Ya'll know they are real right? Well, if not, let me explain exactly what a soul tie is. Soul ties are an emotional or spiritual connection that you have developed for a certain individual; unfortunately, it's usually a fuckboy. Soul ties can be formed on a social, mental, physical or emotional level. These situationships, as I like to call them, grip your heart like a vice grip and won't let you go no matter how many people you date or think you have fallen in love with after the fact.

Some people say that these types of connections are not real and the ones experiencing them have abandonment issues or just simply issues letting go of people, but I know from my own experience that the thing about a soul tie is that you truly feel like you are connected to that person and feel like you're being held hostage. These ties can cause more damage than you know. You can literally feel that person. They can silently drain your mental health without you knowing it.

This could be tempting, like a good thing to some people, but in an actual sense, it could mean a curse in its own way. I've had a soul tie break me down to the point of feeling so numb that I didn't care about the pain and actually welcomed the thought of it because I developed the idea that this is what I deserved. Let me break it down in a way that you will understand what I mean.

Having a connection to someone that feels like it's holding your heart tight doesn't mean that the feelings are reciprocated. Most often, women develop stronger feelings and love harder than the person they are connected to. And in most instances, that person will have no problem talking to other people, but they will inevitably come to profess their so-called undying love for you when they feel the tie breaking. They'll tell you how much they can't live without you and how you mean the whole world to them. The lies honey.

They might even show this through actions, so you get this feeling that they do love you just to string you along a little longer. When you finally realize that this isn't it and start moving on to bigger and healthier things, here comes that "hey bighead" or "I miss you text" just to throw you off again even though they have no intention of ever being with you. I call them Futures. Yes, like the rapper Future. His ill-treatment of women is no secret. They will make themselves appear so pitiful that it becomes difficult for you to leave them alone.

There is a married couple that I know. The husband loves his wife. He does everything within his capacity to make her happy. In fact, if you look at their marriage as an outsider, you would naturally crave to have a marriage like theirs because they look like a match made in heaven. They both understand each other even without saying a word, but this man cheats on his wife constantly. Despite all of the love that they claim to have for one another, he still goes out of his way to cheat on her all of the time. It went unnoticed for a while until it became too hard for him to keep it hidden. It shook their marriage. She wanted a divorce, but he refused to let go; he put her in a situation where leaving him became damn near impossible because they were tied.

All of the attempts that she made to get him out of her life were futile because he tightened his grip on her more and more every time she tried to leave. The divorce didn't go through; even to this day, he isn't faithful to her. The bond that she feels draws her to him despite how he treats her. This is one way to discern who is a fuckboy; they will never want to let go of a good thing and want to have their cake and eat it too. They will suck the life out of you and possess your soul, yet, they won't want to change.

Cheating is not the only angle that we can view a soul tie. It is quite common to see people experiencing mental or physical abuse going on in relationships. Even now, a lot of women are standing up and refusing to be subjected to it and yet a lot of women are still victims of some form of abuse. Despite how rampant it is in many situations; it is surprising that we don't hear about it more often. You would be surprised if people started actually speaking out about what they've endured in a relationship. Some people that we view as role models have been victims of domestic violence, but why do people not talk about it?

Why do people always keep quiet and not speak out when they have been abused by the men who claim to love them? The answer is that people have come to accept that not speaking out is the norm. People believe that a good relationship should be such that the partners should endure when they are treated badly like the previous generations. There is a lot of pretense going on in regards to men thinking that black women need to just shut up and be submissive. We are constantly stereotyped on the premise that we are too loud and "ghetto." This most certainly can put a strain on the expectations or views of how a relationship is supposed to be. Men who date outside of their race ironically bash their own race to prove this point.

Most relationships now are all about whoever can pretend the best. If you can pretend more than the other, then your marriage appears more successful.

Pretending has gradually become the code of conduct in our society. And that is perfect for some because there are a lot of delusional people in this world. We look at celebrities and think of "goals", but in actuality, they may be suffering in silence. A few well-known famous couples have recently been put into the spotlight for the same reason.

Every morning they put on their makeup, their expensive clothes, jewelry, and then get into their expensive car, which was bought by their abusive spouse, and pretend. They always seem happy in public. They never fail to seize any available opportunity to pose for the camera. They will make people believe that they are the happiest people on earth, although they are dying inside.

After they are done showing off for everyone to see, they will return home and be beaten up or are verbally/mentally abused by the same person everyone thinks that they are so happy with. It continues this way until something bad happens. Some women get fed up at some point and decide that they are going to leave because that wasn't part of the love that they were promised, but a fuckboy will make it hard for her to let go or they leave and end up coming back. Soul ties can do anyone like this.

Another soul tie characteristic involves jealousy to the point that they can't let you breathe and don't want to see you happy with anyone else. They believe they love you deeply, and for this reason, they feel like they consistently deserve to be a part of your life and will try to stick around. They see you doing good and have to pop up at your best moments to bring you back down to the "memories" that you have with them. Some crazies use threats as a tactic to stay relevant. There's always that one who will threaten to commit suicide, but the truth is that if you leave them, they will be just fine.

Mental health is a factor that most of us do not think about. We know about our own but not the mentality or how others truly feel. If a man is willing to hurt themselves, then they would hurt you. If you leave, don't look back no matter what they say. Leaving a relationship that isn't benefiting you is the ultimate sign of strength, and no one can take that power away from you. I have a story to tell you about this later.

People with a possessive mindset view others as their property and will always believe that if it is mine, it belongs to me. I can use it however I like, and no one has the right to take it away from me; not even you have the right to take yourself away from me; sounds familiar like a terrible two-year-old. Men or women who see you as their property are those who can and will suffocate you. Their jealousy is next to none. Keep in mind that soul ties don't always come from just the opposite sex.

We must always remember that some are very good with words. They will find the sweetest words that they know will melt your heart but don't allow them to get to you. From my perspective, the problem is not that crazy ass fuckboys just want to feel in control; they may not see you as good enough for them to give their best to yet, but they still won't let you go for the person that is worth you being with. They want to know everything about you so they can use it against you in the long run. Some people who know about your family life and traumatizing events don't want to know for the sake of goodness, red flag. Pay attention.

Especially if they don't want you to know the details of their personal life. You continue staying until one day you wake up and realize that your life has been messed up beyond the point of repair mentally, physically, emotionally, financially, or more. You realize that so many things have gone wrong in your life. Most of us who end up being with a narcissistic person over a long time end up having self-esteem issues. This is because they have lost their self-worth slowly over an extended period of time without realization.

Crazy fuckboys are just out there to destroy your life and make a mess of your growth. Most people who have been involved with narcissistic people for a long time find that they may have lost the will to grow. Narcissists are always threatened by your growth, and they don't want you to achieve more than them because they fear you might break away from their dominance, so they keep you immobile in a sense.

Most often than not, after you leave a stagnant relationship, you realize that your life is dormant and exactly where it was before you met them. In worst cases, you might even find that it has moved backward from what it used to be before you met them and allowed them into your life. Real men water you and watch you flourish.

One of my soul ties was insecure. He was a jealous person who would complain whenever he saw me or any girl with whom he was in a relationship or having a conversation with someone else. His jealousy was so intense that he abused the women in his life mentally, sometimes physically. His problem was that he had anger issues and wouldn't admit that he struggled to control them.

He had a bad experience with a woman in the past that he thought he would end up getting married to, but he caught her cheating weeks after he gave her a ring. As a result of this experience, his insecurities came into play. After that, he was always the jealous type, so much so that whenever he saw any woman that he was with in any type of innocent interaction with another man, such as coworkers, friends, or even family members, he would turn into the crazy nigga. These are the type that cheat and you see them and their girl have a joint social media account. Fuckboys can dish out pain but do not want the same happening to them.

After sharing your password with them, you might start noticing that you can't find some of your friends. It is either they blocked them or kicked them off of your friend list. Whenever they see a guy whom they feel threatened by, all hell breaks loose. Even if you don't have anything to do with whoever DM'ed you trying to holla, they also know that you don't have anything to do with the people inboxing you, but of course, they have little miss scallywag texting them, so they feel guilty and want to project that on someone else.

My situationship was that type of person. He used his past to play on my emotions and make me feel bad for him and want to be there for him. I never was in an actual relationship with him, but I still developed strong feelings for him. I was young and brainless at the time. Luckily, I came to my senses, got older and wiser, and dodged that bullet.

The truth about fuckboys that fall under this category is that they can't see what they do wrong until it's too late. They complain about every woman they were with previously and can never seem to stay in a relationship for long. They blame them for everything that has gone wrong in their lives. To them, every woman that has come into their lives was the cause of their misfortune and failure. Every woman that has been in their life was there to hurt them, but in actuality, they are the ones with the real problem.

They need help, but they fail to see it. Most of the men who complain every chance they get about how badly they were treated in past relationships are usually men who would benefit from going to therapy. Although some of them, therapy would not help and they need to go get a lobotomy if you ask me. There is a major stigma about therapy in most ethnic communities.

It is viewed as weak or weird. I don't know how this became normalized, but it has to stop. If you are the person that thinks they are always right and everyone else is crazy, chances are, you need an SSI check! If everyone around you keeps having issues that involve you, perhaps there is a problem that you cannot see and are not taking into consideration. Everybody cannot be against just you all of the time. Everyone tends to have a hater or two, but the whole world hates you? Like Boosie would say, "C'mon mane." The truth is that when everyone is hating or complaining, you should look at the person in the mirror and decide whether or not what they're saying is true or how to fix the problem.

The wisest people on earth are people that are good at making observations. They didn't get this way by running their mouth or jumping to conclusions prematurely. They are also not quick to judge other people. Whenever there is an issue, they take their time to observe. They look carefully to analyze everything. After careful scrutinization, they find out the main cause of the problem and attempt to fix it.

When people constantly complain about something that involves you and you notice that people continue leaving because of the very thing which they keep complaining about, you need to learn to sit back and observe. Is what they are saying true? The main reason why some people find it difficult to reflect on their behavior is that they already have it in mind that they are right.

I know quite a few people that are completely off of their rocker, but to them, that is not the case; it's us. There has never been anybody in the world that was born without an imperfection. Some of these imperfections we find in our lives come in accordance with bad habits we've built up in the course of going through certain things in life that we don't want to relive or discuss out of fear. Fear of being judged, embarrassed, or ridiculed because we knew that we knew better. One thing that you can do if you care about a person and see them struggling to unravel their thoughts is to suggest therapy and maybe they will flat out refuse, but keep planting those seeds.

They have it in mind that no one has their best interest at heart. People who are infallibly angry at criticism, especially when the criticism is done in the right way, are those that never want to change from their toxic way of thinking. If you want to change for the better, you have to be completely open and honest with yourself. Fuckboys, unfortunately, do not have this type of common sense. They might be able to take themself out of the crazy fuckboy category if or when they decide to work on themself.

Let me make it clearer, being crazy is not something that is assumingly a bad thing. We all have a little bit of crazy, whether we like to admit it or not. The difference is that some people know when they are being crazy and others don't. I know people that are viewed as crazy in a way that they are caring towards others but neglect themselves. Others are crazy to the extent of staying in a relationship because they feel that this type of unforgiving love is what they deserve. At the end of the day, we have all done things that we are not proud of. Even the president, who is the chief security officer, could decide to make an immoral decision if they so wished to.

All of the above-mentioned people often develop some habits that make them imperfect. Most of these habits became so imminent in their lives and thought processes that they feel that they have to accept to be this way and that this "is just the way that I am." But one good thing about life is that we have free will, morals, and values. Everybody has some degree of crazy in them. There is nobody that is immune to having bad intentions and if they say they are, it's a lie and I would stay as far away from that loon as possible.

|4|
MILITARY

Military men are also fuckboys, not all of them though. I was in the military for twelve years, and I witnessed all types of fuckery dealing with the ones that were. You would not believe the things I have seen some of them do. Not only did I date them, I had to be around a ton of them daily so I learned how they work all too well. They are the ones who would roll up in their Challengers, Chargers, and Mustangs selling dreams with a fresh side of fun and tall tales. They are very conscious of their appearance. No, for real, they dress so damn good and want anyone's attention. Or they are the opposite and can't dress, like those men who you can tell got their outfit straight off a mannequin looking like a fruit basket. They have the freshest haircuts and jewelry, and most of the time, they'll even have expensive clothes on, but usually would be sleeping on their friend's couch.

One thing that I noticed about them is that they prioritize their appearance more than other things that really matter. I see them as people who prefer to chase after fairytales while selling you one. They put on a life of having it all, and spend their money on material things just to look fly, but in actuality, they don't even have a place to stay or they stay in government housing. Yes, I said government housing, the barracks. There's nothing wrong with it, but instead of getting a decent place to stay, they'd rather spend their money on Jordans and cars that they know damn well they can not afford just to pull up to the club then leave and return to their friend's couch to sleep every night. They can barely afford to buy a woman a single drink or put gas in their car.

People who live outside of their means are scary to me. They attempt to make the impression that they are in their bag, running it up, but in actuality, they are broke-ass niggas who live fake lives and use their money to show off, perhaps with the intention of looking for a woman to turn into their prey.

I could tell you guys a million stories of my interactions with these fools but one incident, in particular, stands out. I was 19 at the time and fresh out of basic training with the best body of my entire life. I met this guy at Army training. Let's just call him Terrance; I can't tell ya'll his real name. Terrance was suave as fuck. He was from a certain state in the south that gave him an accent that could make your heart melt. He had caramel skin, in shape, with the waves on point. At the time, I was young and I didn't know then, but these were all signs of a fuckboy.

Not to say that every man with such characteristics is a fuckboy, but the majority, I would say, are fuckboys. I was a nerd, the type that had no business trying to square up with Terrance. I was just standing there, being my socially awkward self, and that's when he approached me licking his lips and being all slick. I think I fell for it right then. In the military service that I was in, we had to train for one weekend a month and every drill weekend; guess who was right on my ass or in my face? It was Terrance.

All of the other people in my unit warned me beforehand to leave his ass alone, but I wouldn't listen and was a hopeless romantic. They already saw what I was too blind to see at the time. Terrance was the biggest liar that I have met in my entire life; most military niggas are. That's another observation that I made during my time serving. The thing about being in a situation like this is that red flags can look like the most exciting ride at Six Flags and I was not ready at all. But I said to myself, "let me ride every roller coaster in this park," not really knowing that I would be the one getting thrown for a loop.

Terrance told me that he moved upstate because of a natural disaster and got separated from his family. He stated that he did not know if they were dead or alive and I felt so bad. I should have questioned this back then, but I was mesmerized by this man or whom I presumed at the time to be a man. Some people grew up in a bad environment. They've grown up watching one parent abuse the other or one or both of their parents may have abused them mentally, physically, or emotionally and they are destined to abuse people as they grow older unless they break the cycle. I'm sure If I had asked questions, I would have insight into how fucked up he truly was.

Fast forward along to another point in my military career, I had advanced to become a recruiter assistant while Terrance got an active duty job in the same city and had to drive an hour from where he lived to work every day. And what did I take it upon myself to do? My dumbass invited him to come to stay with me.

Things were cool for a few months, and I still didn't question him too much about his family. That may have partially contributed to my ending up in this situation with him. If you feel like something isn't right, ask questions and if they don't want to answer them yea, they're on some fuck shit. However, our unit was getting ready to deploy to Iraq, and I volunteered to go. Little did I know that I was pregnant at the time. I thought he would be excited, but he was so mad, and I could not understand why. His explanation was that he didn't want everyone in the unit to know. Wild right?

We lived together every day, and he didn't want them to know? I was floored. So, here I am, pregnant and unable to go overseas with a child that he didn't want. Things could not get much worst, right? Wrong! I thought about things at that point, and my intuition started gearing up. I felt like there was some stuff that he wasn't telling me. I went through his phone, which is something I never do and discovered that this man had a whole other life going on.

I knew that he had a daughter, but he said that his baby mama died in the natural disaster with the rest of his family, Hurricane Katrina, to be specific, so I kind of felt bad for him. I ended up self-destructing to the point where I could not recognize myself and ended up having a miscarriage due to all the stress that he caused. This was an interesting point in my life because I always struggled with negative body image and depression. My depression went to an all-time-high after this one.

I ended up deploying overseas with him and my unit after all. While we were in Iraq, he proceeded to cheat on me with any and everybody on base despite the situation that I was in. I caught him once and was so angry, but why? I knew he was not worth my time, but he would always apologize. The final straw for me was when I discovered his baby mama was alive and well, so I messaged her on Myspace.

He was enraged when he found out and said that I should have kept my mouth shut because she wrecked his car, a Mustang, imagine that and that she was going to put him on child support. This man forgot my birthday every year and never appreciated anything I ever did, but I was the one in the wrong. I believe that he deserved every bit of it.

I couldn't help but feel dumb knowing that I fell for every single one of this chronic liar's tricks and ended up looking like a fool. I cooked for him and did everything, but alas, life just happened. I believe every dog has its day. I continued to see Terrance from time to time, and it took a long time to get over him, but I am definitely glad that I finally did. There will be men who when women treat them the best way they can, they will return the favor by treating them awfully. Just imagine if I would've gotten stuck with him.

I felt helpless for a long time after that experience and wondered why he didn't love or care about me like I did him. The hardest lesson that I have had to learn in life is that feelings aren't always reciprocated by everyone that you encounter and happen to fall in love with. I ended up in many situationships expecting the same loyalty that I provided from people who just could not give the same in return. We as women tend to do this, give ourselves away to men who know how to do nothing more than take and end up with egg on our face while they continue on with their lives scott free. Unbeknownst to them, the permanent damage that they have caused to someone else. I often wonder if they reconsider or regret hurting someone. At the end of the day, I highly doubt it.

Most of those that end up finding themselves in a difficult situation, have you ever asked yourself, how did I let this happen? Let's take, for example, that there are currently hundreds of thousands of people in the hospital undergoing chemotherapy. These people never asked to be diagnosed with cancer. Some are healthy adults who haven't smoked, eaten right, or have never done anything unhealthy a day in their lives yet still have a life-altering disease. Does anyone ask for these types of things to happen?

When you think about it deeply, you will see that the answer is a clear 'NO.' I'm in no way, shape, form, or fashion comparing the severity of such a serious illness to a fuckboy just trying to prove the point that we often end up going through things accidentally. Another example can be cited from people that happen to find themselves as victims of a car accident due to the carelessness of a drunk driver or someone not paying attention because they're too busy texting.

They wake up in the morning and have already planned things that they would like to accomplish for the day. They decide to venture out, but along the lines, they find themselves at the wrong place at the wrong time. Drunk drivers never intend to hit people, but because they are impaired, they do and can ruin or alter someone else's life forever. When you look at the people involved in the accident, it wasn't something they wanted for themselves; they never planned it. They ended up finding themselves as a victim because of someone else's negligent decision to get behind the wheel drunk.

I do not agree that all fuckboys intend to hurt people, although some do because ya'll know the age-old saying that hurt people, hurt people. Their way of thinking makes their desire to fuck people over inevitable. The ones that don't do it on purpose are most likely shallow idiots who don't think about how their decisions can affect others. They can't help it like cavemen who have to pound on things with their clubs.

Some of them may end up thinking about the consequences of their action and then some of them do not give a single care. Most shallow-minded people out there don't want to hurt anyone but still have a motive just the same. They often act before they think. Whenever they are faced with a situation, they act according to their personality, which tends to be destructive as was my experience with Terrance. I am so glad that I dodged that one as well.

|5|
THE NICE GUY

Do nice people always finish last? That may be true, but in this case, we are referring to the ones who pretend that their mothers have installed manners in them, which may be the case, but their sole purpose in life is to waste women's time until they find exactly what they are looking for. They may seem genuine, open doors, and say all of the right things that gentlemen do, but passively-aggressively tear you down or orchestrate you in ways your brain cannot comprehend. They are nothing to play with, and their weapon of choice is their ability to apologize; believe it or not, that's what it is.

Although this might seem like a harmless trait, even thoughtful or wonderful at times, these nice guys are one of the most dangerous to encounter. Their charm is second to none. Many fuckboys can use chameleon-like techniques to disguise their ways, but this one will deceive you every single time. These ninjas will apologize when they are wrong and hell might even apologize when you are wrong. They definitely aren't coming into your life to help you build sis. A man that comes into your life to build with you wouldn't apologize when you are wrong. He would correct you without tearing you down and secretly trying to manipulate you.

As I already said, even good people have some degree of crazy in them, but they still do good; why? Because they have limits. They have that boundary set in their lives that determines the limit they must never exceed in whatever they choose to do or how they choose to associate with people. Good people have limits. They have things that they believe they will never do, especially when they are things that will end up hurting others. They don't even need to think about those things in which they will never do because the act of not doing it has naturally become part of them over the years. It seems like common sense. But common sense ain't always so common.

As for a fuckboy, they have no limit to the length they can go to make someone's life become miserable. They have no limit to the bullshit that they are ready to cause you. Once you give them the opportunity to come into your life, they end up messing everything up for you, and they turn your life around in the wrong direction with their lack of limits towards hurting others whether they intend to or not.

Fuckboys often lead girls into believing that they are special and they care so much about them, then they literally turn into Dr. Jekyll to do whatever they can to get laid or to get whatever it is they want at the particular time from someone. And again, once he wants something from you, you better believe he will do all that he can to get that very thing and put the paws on you. In some particular instances, they may even be able to confuse you and even themselves by thinking that they are really nice people if you happen to be the person whom they intend to get something from.

A fuckboy has no honor once it comes to getting what he wants. As long as whatever he is doing is helping him get it, he will go to any length to do whatever he believes will get him the object that he desires. A person that can do just about anything to get what they want is an alarming one. This has nothing to do with pride.

Let's take, for example, when a fuckboy wants to fuck, and his woman is not in a position at the time to give him any for whatever reason, they will naturally look for anyone that is available at that time to get it regardless of who it is. That's how some of them end up with more kids than Nick Cannon, multiple ratchet baby mamas, and expect you to play stepmama to all of them if they even take care of them, tuh. Real men will wait. Charlamagne Tha God once made the statement that "black men don't cheat." This may be true to some extent and this is where the boys are separated from real men; but needless to say, not all men are faithful.

A real man knows that this is not a good look. He respects his woman and would have to either get hold of the urge or wait for the right moment. As for a fuckboy, he ain't waiting, simple as that. Once he sees another woman that seems available, he is without a shadow of a doubt, going to try it. Sure every guy has urges to look at other women, there is nothing wrong with it like we discussed before. The problem lies in having the inability to be monogamous. Whenever a fuckboy happens to not cheat, it is mainly because he lacks the opportunity to cheat.

Once an opportunity presents itself, he takes it immediately and will do it. I believe cheating on your partner is one of the coldest things one would ever dare do to do, but who am I to say? If someone is actually in love with you and they are able to look at every other person around and decide to choose you, it shows how much value they have for you. It is not just about choosing you; they decided that it is either you or no one else.

Monogamy isn't for everyone. Some people choose polyamory and that's ok too. But that's not for everybody either. I get so sick and tired of hearing men say they want multiple women but can't even deal with one nor do they have the financial stability or mental capacity to support this theory. But that's a story for another day as well.

Women are more likely to stay faithful in a relationship. Don't quote me on this, but we often have many admirers, people that want to be something more than friends but decide to hold on to the one person that we care about, even if that means getting hurt. We tend to believe in the person we are with and believe in every single one of their dreams and hopes, no matter how farfetched. That's how it's supposed to be. Letting go of anyone who has that type of love for you would be a big mistake.

We also support our partners in every aspect when we care, but as a fuckboy, they end up not seeing any of this at all. As you clearly know, when someone is doing all these wonderful things just because of you, instead of reciprocating all that, they decide to take advantage of the vulnerability without a single regard. I think men who love their women would never dare cheat on them, but then again it's not uncommon.

If someone loves you enough to break every barrier and cut every tie just to be with you, they deserve every degree of faithfulness that you have to offer; they deserve the highest form of respect a person should receive from their significant other. Loyalty is something fuckboys don't want to provide. Even though they know about all that you have done for them, they still go out of their way to do crazy shit just because.

So, for some odd reason, we meet nice guys at a time in life when things may or may not be going so well. In the end, they strike like a scorpion when you least expect it. After all of the time that they spent being so sweet and uplifting, chances are that they were doing some foul shit behind your back. This is where the word loyalty comes into play again. The catch with these fuckboys is that they weren't pretending to be nice, they are nice, but they are still fuckboys nonetheless. I like to think of Lawrence and Issa's situation on the HBO show, "Insecure." Some people might be confused about what I mean when I say that some super nice guys are fuckboys but the story that unfolded in this show is a classic example of a seemingly nice man being a fuckboy.

A similar set of circumstances happened to someone that I know that can provide another clear explanation of what I mean. She met this guy on an online dating site. They conversed often and decided to meet offline. On the day of their first face-to-face date, the guy couldn't make it, but didn't give her a reason. He kept apologizing so, she gave him another chance.

They set up a day for another date, and it was amazing. She was reluctant to meet the asshole that bailed out on her for their date at first, but he turned out to be a decent man. He showed a lot of potential so they decided to take it to the next level. They got into a relationship. He was the single-handedly, most genuine, affectionate guy that she had ever met. Most of the men that she met before always found it difficult to apologize whenever they were wrong or treated her badly but not this one. He didn't only unnecessarily apologize. He was sincere and a true gentleman or so she thought.

Women sometimes think of gentlemen as a knight in shining armor type. These are the best kind of men to date, although rare. So, of course, when you think that you have one, hold on to them. She did just that and thought that she had found one. They dated for months and were almost dating for a year when one particular night, she figured out that he didn't feel the same way that she felt about him even after all the time that they had spent together. It was devastating. Looking into the situation more, she found out that he had been married before he met her, they had kids, and were still married. She confronted him because he had never told her. His response was that he didn't think it was necessary to tell her because they were separated.

Baby, boo, if those divorce papers aren't final, then please take heed.

Needless to say, the divorce never happened. When she asked him again, he gave the excuse that he was stalling because his wife was sick and couldn't work. He said that him and his lawyer were preparing paperwork to go through with it and get full custody of the children she had no idea about at first but now wasn't the right time. Yet he was still so genuine that she believed every word that he said.

The only issue that she had with him was the other woman. She ended up in a situationship with him for two whole years after she met him. His wife was also somehow still in the picture. No matter how nice a person may seem, at some point in time, you realize that you have to make a decision for yourself.

His wife, already knew that he is dealing with another woman as well, but he continued to treat them both well. She trusted him just as much as my friend did because he was able to put on this facade of having everyone's best interest at heart and took care of both households. These are signs that no one can often see through. If someone is too good to be true, chances are that they are.

That's not always the case, but when she eventually found out that he had a wife, of course, she didn't leave like she should have but she thought that she had finally met the man of her dreams that she deserved. These men never change; he still wanted her to continue being in his life and never stopped being pleasant but would not commit to her alone. You have to watch out for these men. They may seem authentic but, in actuality, are a typical fuckboy.

We tend to get caught up in our significant other's endeavors by default because we often times don't have a choice. When in a mutual relationship, it's not uncommon for us to go with the flow and to let our men lead. Evolution took a major turn for the greater when women were allowed to vote. This point in history is where things got interesting and more women started to become independent. Those forced to deal with the regular patriarchal type of environment eventually started learning how to stand up for themselves, which is frowned upon.

Back in the day, women kept quiet and weren't allowed to freely express their wants, needs, and desires. The norm was to be quiet. The truth is that there were more successful marriages back in the day than there are now for this reason. People talk about it all the time and stay comparing marriages to then and now. It is a known fact that now there is a higher divorce rate. Some would even argue that marriages were better then as opposed to now. The reason why marriages were better and lasted longer was because women around that time period were only faced with only one option.

Some marriages back then were often one-sided and never about teamwork. Betty would have 30 chirren and take care of the home while George went out and worked because she had no choice. She had to accept it without complaining. If she complained, society saw her as a bad wife or as a bad influence on others; society saw her as someone that has deviated from doing what they termed as 'being right.' A woman rarely had a say in how things went in her household. And that being a good wife entailed being quiet and taking whatever shitty treatment came from the man that she called her husband. Some were lucky enough, but at some point, I'm sure that they endured some form of abuse, and since their friend next door had it worse or they had no means to support themselves or their children, they tolerated it. Silence was expected back then.

The truth was that marriages weren't really working. They were just barely hanging on. They were seemingly nice because the women involved were forced into them by family at a young age, had to keep quiet, and put up with every form of abuse thrown at them by the men that were supposed to love them. That's not love to me.

No one wanted to be seen as a bad wife. Once you got married, you became obligated to do whatever your spouse asked you to do. It didn't matter whether what they were asking her to do made sense or not. It didn't even matter whether what he was asking her to do made her look stupid. The standard was that she was going to do it, and if she ended up refusing to do it, she would be labeled as being disobedient like Ceily from "The Color Purple." Shouldn't the word 'disobedient' be used between a parent and a child or by a pet owner? Of course, marriage isn't a situation between a child and an adult.

People should rather be asked to respect their partners than obey them. As a result of how disgusting some marriages were then, so many women were and are living in denial til this day because it has been passed down to them generation after generation. This is why some older women say that you should stay in a relationship that isn't worth saving.

Some of them had things they wanted their partner to do differently, but because of the norm, they couldn't speak about it. So, they remained quiet. Some women had to fake being happy and orgasms just to hide the fact that their needs were not met. We are definitely known for faking orgasms.

Women were more at risk of cheating during those days because even when they couldn't get good sex from their significant other, they would have to pretend that he was doing it right. Their husbands were gone the majority of the time and, most often times than not, were out cheating on them too. So who wouldn't contemplate not having a sneaky link all while pretending like they are being satisfied and that fine-looking milkman was knocking on the door every day? Not me.

The norm made it almost impossible for them to be able to express themselves sexually, even down to how they dressed. Everyone has their own deviant thoughts. Some people don't like to admit it and some people, even now try to make it a point to make others feel bad for using a toy every now and again. When it comes to wanting who or what you want if you don't please yourself who will? So go ahead and buy that rose sex toy if you want to girl.

There were men that were and there are men today that are still very loving towards the women in their lives though. These men allowed their women to be part of the decision-making for their families. They did their best to live their lives differently, away from the things that were going on around them. In the end, these men's marriages became what so many people around them were envious to have. These are the type of long-lasting marriages that I think of when asked my opinion about the good ol' days.

The ones that are so pressed about those being the best times wouldn't be able to hold a candle to what those men did to make their marriage last. So many men saw taking advantage of women as their right and felt entitled. That isn't the case today. Although this way of thinking has attempted to trickle down and rear its ugly head in society again. This is one of the many reasons why I disagree that past marriages were better in comparison. Marriage is definitely not for the weak and is not the ultimate goal for everyone. But imagine ending up being with someone who didn't satisfy you or was unattractive.

I wouldn't argue with the fact that marriages then lasted longer than they do today. This is a fact that we can't dispute, but saying that women back then were better wives is something that I wouldn't totally agree with. They had expectations established at birth and their sole purpose was to become a wife. Women today choose not to be married more often than not, regardless of how peers and family view them.

Since the beginning of time, when a woman decides to do things her way, she gets viewed or labeled as enemy number one. We got called harlots, jezebels, and witches burned at the stake just for having our own beliefs and opinions. Any woman marked with the "scarlet letter" had many stigmas associated with her. My question is, why is it that women are expected to be the bigger person in a relationship where two people are supposed to be a team? Why should a woman be the only one required to listen and communicate effectively?

Just as a man has his own free will, women weren't allowed to do the same. Just as a man grew up in a certain environment and was allowed to do things because "boys will be boys," that doesn't excuse the fact that no one should be treated as an object. We all socialized with different people and got exposed to life in one way or another. Not trying to get on my feminist soapbox high horse, but who decided that men were better?

There have always been a ton of fuckboys around. Women from previous generations were humiliated and treated awful, but they remained quiet and continued smiling in public even when they were actually crying in secret. But now, everything has changed.

At some point, you could wake up one morning and hear on the news that someone whom you thought had the best marriage ever was murdered by her husband or maybe snapped and killed him. Everything that glitters is not gold. Til death do you part.

One truth that we don't learn until we are older is that there are many women going through the same issues that we are. So many people have been abused in their lifetime, but refuse to come forward and speak out against it because it is painful or embarrassing. Sometimes being quiet and suffering in silence seems like the only solution. Again, this is why a lot of people choose to avoid therapy.

We were known to be submissive and docile, but now we have women to look up to that spoke out and paved the way for us to be great today. The US has roughly 12.3 million women-owned businesses; on average, those businesses tend to grow more rapidly. The number of women who hold college degrees is astounding; with that being said, what would be the point of struggling internally trying to juggle life, a family, and your own mental health on top of dating a fuckboy? We have figured out that when we do give fuckboys an inch, they are almost always going to try to take a million miles. It never fails. I've run across a few fuckboys in my day that wanted nothing more than financial support.

These are commonly pretty boys and the type that call any female with a good job "big money." It is embarrassing to think that a man would want to be financially supported by a woman but not unlikely at all. I wonder if these are the types raised by a woman who grew up scamming and finessing people their whole lives, so of course, monkey see, monkey do. They see dollar signs and immediately think that they hit a lick or have found a sugar mama. Fuckboys love these types of games.

Most women are now learning to be strong. We have learned that the world is a very harsh, unforgiving place. Normally, those seen as the strong should protect those seen as the weak, but this has rarely been the case in the world that we live in today.

Yet, nobody can be blamed for just wanting a nice person in their lives. Nobody wants to willingly be involved with someone that you know would end up just being a waste of time. They always appear to be the nicest people on earth. If we all had crystal balls and knew that our ex would end up treating us the way he did, I am almost one hundred percent certain things would have gone in a completely different direction. And most women now prefer to remain single than to endure the pains associated with dating. This is where many men in this century have come up with the term 'feminism."

They claim that women are now too independent and emit too much masculine energy to be able to keep a man anyway. In light of recent events involving a certain man named Kevin Samuels who claimed to be a dating expert, it was placed on the board that women should not be choosey on who they date if they are not high value themselves. I did not do much reading on his beliefs, but I know that this misogynistic way of thinking helps contribute to the pee in the dating pool today.

|6|
THE MAMA'S BOY

Everyone loves their mama, right? Well, not everyone, but most do to a certain extent, and some to an extreme extent that it is almost incestuous, but no one wants to talk about this subject because it's super fucking weird. Mothers are placed on earth to nurture their children and show them the way until they are able to care for themselves. They are meant to make good decisions for their children until they are old enough to make sound decisions for themselves. It is the same with every other species of animal. Yet we as humans hold onto our children for 18 years, the longest amount of time of any mammal on earth. Even after adulthood, some children need various forms of extra support or nurturing, and that is what mothers are known for.

So despite most of us being cared for until we are eighteen, if we are fortunate enough to do so, there are a few certain individuals who will end up sucking on their mother's tit for the rest of their entire lives because she allows them to. This is a mama's boy... And oh my god, they are annoying and sick like their mothers.

Most mothers grasp the concept that their offspring have to leave the nest, but there are a select few that will never let their precious sons go and will ruin every single relationship he is in, some on purpose and some passively. All family dynamics are different and everyone is brought up differently as well. In certain communities, it is commonly portrayed as a single mother raising a son to be an image of whom she fantasizes about dating. Or that she is raising her "King."

The only problem with this is that they coddle their sons and don't realize how this has a negative impact on them and how they will treat women in the future. Let's take Future, for example again, he is the epitome of what we would call a fuckboy, and I often wonder how his mother feels about how he views women because she never makes the effort to try and rectify the behavior.

Mama's boys have been trained to never make any decision in their lives without the consent of their mothers. This means that their mom gets a full update of whatever is happening in their life, whoever they meet, how they meet, and just about every other aspect of their relationship and life. Whatever their mom asks them to do, without hesitation, even whether what she asked them to do was the right thing for them or was something that would cost them their happiness. These boys are grossly manipulated by their mothers. Some of them would prefer to continue living with their moms, but even those who aren't living with them are essentially still living with their mom since she still has her thumb on him. Whenever a woman comes into the life of a mama's boy, you might as well prepare yourself to be dating the both of them.

Whatever happens in his relationship, she gets every detail about it and is always the one to suggest what he should do whenever there is an issue. His mom has more say so in his life than he does. In fact, he has no say in his life. Whatever his mom decides, that's exactly what he does because she is the subject matter expert even though these are the women that usually couldn't even keep a man to save their own life.

If you somehow end up marrying a mama's boy, you best believe that there is never a secret between him and his precious mama. She will know all of your business because he tells her everything, the good, the bad, and the ugly. If you can't cook, he's snitching. If you can't do laundry, she will know, and maybe if you aren't that great in bed shoot he might even tell her that too!

The one thing that is the most annoying about a mama's boy is that his mom ALWAYS has a favorite ex that he dated in the past and of course, it's not you, and she will let you know every chance that she gets. Some overbearing mothers are indirect others are more boisterous because they would rather not see their precious baby boy with the likes of you. His mom decides how he treats every female in his life, and she also makes the major decision on how the relationship is run.

Any woman that ends up with a mama's boy will regret it unless you have the patience of a saint. We are natural-born healers and nurturers, but there are some things that we draw the line at. They are one of the worst kinds of fuckboys because despite how amazing your relationship is there is always this one jealous entity, his mama, that's out there secretly competing with you to ruin the relationship, and they are unable to see it. The red flag here comes in with them invariably talking about their mom. This is how you will be able to spot them.

Yes, they always talk about their mom. Now it isn't bad for one to always bring up their mother, but if you're smart, you should know that this appears to arise from some in-depth issues that will only get worse as time passes if you stick around. I've seen those posts on TikTok about who should a man put first his mom, wife, or daughter. Regardless of what you think or who should get served their plate first, this nigga is, on every occasion, going to choose his mom, so there's no use of you even voicing your concern. You could cook and clean every day, but if it's not like his mom's, he will turn his nose up at it.

This type of fuckboy can be controlling without even realizing it. They enjoy being the decision maker in the relationship. Do as I say, not as I do. If you notice that someone has started trying to make decisions for you or make you feel crazy, that is a major red flag too. Their signature move is to try to make you feel worthless. To them, they are more important than you, and so are their wants and needs. They want you to baby them. Imagine a grown man stuck on being a kid. There are plenty of them out there.

In order to thrive and continue to form a stable relationship, respect is one of the main components. I've seen some men go out of their way to disrespect their women. Why, because it's allowed. Any respectful man would show the world how lucky they are to have you. A fuckboy will go out of their way to show you how lucky you are to have them in your life. They will not only try to show you how lucky you are to have them but will constantly remind you of it.

Fuckboys are those people that think they are perfect in all that they do. Any little mistake that you make, oh god, they will remind you, but when you bring up something they've done that magically never happened. Fellas should know by now that most women don't forget anything. We will remember that text on his phone from 2001 that he got 13 seconds before 9/11 happened from the hoe down the street.

Most mama's boys glorify their mother. He sees her as a god over you, the perfect depiction of what a woman should be because she has brainwashed him into thinking so. He sees himself as someone that is meant to be pleased by you, as someone whom you are meant to be under all the time, and as someone that is meant to pilot your life because his mom lets him get away with murder so you should too. Clingy isn't even the word to describe them. They are fuckboys that hardly accept anything you do or say without having a reason to complain about it and how she does it better, which is weird.

They aren't going to cheat on you, or if they do, it would be with their mom's favorite ex and she had something to do with it without a shadow of a doubt. And don't even attempt to be nice to this lady because it's futile. That is why I say his family is not yours. Men like this should just get a sex doll and glue their mom's face on it instead of wasting other women's time. If you want to fuck your mom, just say that!

|7|
DRUG DEALERS

They are the ever-wonderful seller of pharmaceuticals that are well known in neighborhoods that can easily sweep anyone off of their feet, if you are into that type of thing. These days, the number of women to men is 5:1, and everyone is so eager to be in a relationship that anyone who simply provides compliments is the ideal person regardless of their occupation.

My experience with this type was a rather interesting one. I told y'all before that I was a nerd growing up, and I definitely wasn't doing what most other teenage girls my age were doing. We all know that the younger generations fall prey to things that most parents wouldn't want their children to get involved with due to lack of parental guidance, peer pressure, poor judgment or just curiosity. We all lacked knowledge and experience at some point until life came and smacked us in the face with lessons.

Lack of parental guidance is one of the main reasons a lot of people end up making mistakes that turn their lives upside down. There are things kids should normally learn from their parents, but when they fail to be taught, they end up learning from the wrong place and the wrong people who can't or won't teach them the correct way. Again, monkey see, monkey do, but that can be harmful when interacting with the opposite sex. This can definitely make or break you as a young adult. I wish that I had known.

There are many reasons that kids end up finding themselves in situations where they lack supervision. Parents have to work because of how fearful the economy has become and there is no village anymore; this is an unavoidable fact. Everyone is not raised the same either, so some children are forced to grow up fast. As young women, we are told to dress appropriately in front of older men and have all of these rules, yet the older men still lust after younger women because they are easy to control.

We always see cases where a grown-ass man who is old enough to be somebody's dad talking to a teenage girl, they end up getting married then stuck with that person. Growing up, we usually ran into that one oldhead who would hang out at the high school and teen events trying to be seen. Luckily most of us did not fall for their bullshit. But not everyone is so lucky. The ones who do get pressured into relationships with these pedophiles lives' become a total mess and will never be the same. I call them that because that's exactly what they are. Their dreams get cut off because after marrying him, they basically become his prisoner. I've seen it happen growing up, and when I see those women now, they usually have an interesting story to tell about the whole situation.

Peer pressure is another major reason why many lives have become messed up today. Peers are one of the biggest decision-makers in our lives, even as adults. This can be extremely dangerous when a child hasn't been given the necessary tools to think critically or for themselves by an adult figure and are thrown to the wayside. When they need to learn things from their parents and are failed by them, they fall back on their peers, who end up advising them based on their own juvenile experience or from what they have seen or heard. This is why we were always instructed to choose our friends wisely.

Some of us knew if something we were told to do was wrong because we were taught. We hesitated to do it, but our peers continued to mount pressure. Eventually, everyone gives in because so-called "friends" sometimes can make you feel like the odd one, or we would be left out if we didn't follow social trends. Life continues this way even throughout adulthood. A number of people have found themselves involved in gang activity, drug use, or wound up being sent to jail, as a result of which the main cause was peer pressure. A lot of people who smoke weed started when they were younger. 99.9% of the time, their peers pressured them into it and they found out that they enjoyed it, so they continued to do so, but they plausibly never would have tried it if it wasn't for their friends. Tell me I'm lying.

Poor judgment is another reason why people make mistakes in life. Being uneducated on a subject as very young girls or boys leads to falling into the wrong hands. We can't talk about this without talking about curiosity. Curiosity killed the cat. Often times it is why we tried testing our mamas by sneaking out or staying out after curfew and found out how dumb of a decision that turned out to be.

Everyone tends to come to a crossroads at a time in their lives because they are curious. We saw others doing something and then decided to try it out ourselves. Perhaps others that were doing whatever it was had precursors or morals, which had been helping them manage the obstacles of life, but curiosity can, of course, get the better of anyone. Because we are curious by nature, we tend to do things that we have seen others doing without questioning and end up making a mistake that we later regret. This is why I hate the term influencer. It means exactly what the name says. People spend hours and hours making video content, knowing that young people will watch in awe and follow along with what they say aimlessly. Even older people love following social media trends now too. The recipes and life hacks on TikTok always get me.

The twenty-first century has brought us up to revere the ill-treatment of women as well. It has become way too common. Women are viewed as devices. Even to the supreme court, which we know is true based on the decision to overturn the Roe vs. Wade case. In countries you'll visit today, you will still find something like 'honor killing' being carried out against women. Just recently, I was reading the news, and I saw this story about how a girl was killed by her family and her supposed forced groom, just because she refused to accept to marry him and decided to elope with someone else that she actually loved.

The groom, let's just say wasn't the noblest person on the planet. She found out early on, followed her instinct, and rejected him, but he came together with her family and they killed her in the name of an honor killing. When you see things like this happen, you ask yourself, what did women who found themselves in such a situation do to deserve that type of injustice? And it's hard to believe that things like this are still happening in 2022.

All over the world, teens are raped daily in light of sex trafficking and other reasons. These girls ended up trusting someone that didn't mean them any good. The funny thing is people know it's wrong but don't say a single word about it or if they do, they get backlash from others who agree with the situation, which is crazy. I find that a lot of internet trolls agree with the negative side of a view and have no problem letting you know why. Like we even asked for their opinion.

Is there any reasonable excuse to hurt people who never thought of hurting you? Unless you're a doctor or have some occupation of that sort, I don't think there is. They get paid to cause pain and discomfort to people to save their life, but others are out here doing it for free. This is the equivalent of all those fuckboys that go around hurting people that did absolutely nothing to them like the world isn't already a scary enough place. We are always dealing with going through one problem or another without someone adding stress to our situation.

But anyway, back to the fuckboy at hand. The drug dealers. I have a story to tell about this one as well. Young me, who never wanted to fit in, moved to a big city for college from my small town and started going out or showing out rather. A bigger city equaled more parties and trouble to get into. I still never acted like a clout-chasing female though, so remember that. I recall pulling up to the parties late at night, on my quiet Alessia Cara vibes, and observing my surroundings, never knowing that I would ever end up falling for the kind of people that I did.

I was a straight-A student and had a lot of common sense as well, enough to know that no one could pull the wool over my eyes or so I thought. This was until I met a particular person who happened to be a drug dealer. The thing is, most drug dealers can sell water to a fish and are super smooth. I grew up in the country, like horses and cows country and had some street smarts but mine were no match for those of someone who was in the streets on a daily basis.

I met a ton of friends that grew up in the city and we would go out; low and behold here comes some guy pulling up in his nice car (remember we talked about nice cars being the fuckboy trademark) to single my little country ass of all of the others and say something along the lines of, "I like you. You are different." Who doesn't like a compliment from a fine-ass, persuasive man? Most drug dealers are handsome. I don't know why but Jesus they know how to dress, talk, and they always have the best cologne that smells like heaven.

Back to the story, I roll my eyes because I do know that this is basic fuckboy lingo by now, but since I was more reserved and not wilding out like everyone twerking for the attention; it was nice to be noticed for a change. One day, I took the bait and started talking to one. At the time, I did not know this man's occupation and later, when I did find out, it was too late and didn't even matter.

Everyone likes a bad boy who caters to your every whim and he did just that. Y'all know that it is true. It feels like you won some type of award when you are seen out with them and picture yourself being a trophy wife. The thing that made him fit the category of a fuckboy was that he was the biggest manipulator and full of drama. I would get looked at crazy by every female if we went somewhere, and if anyone looked my way, he was going to say something but I never did. Granted he was an attentive guy and had some good dick, but I had no business even trying to be about that life. His phone rang constantly and even after constant reassurance that he was not cheating, he ended up having two females pregnant at the same time, and I was not one of them. This type of situation was definitely one to learn from.

Not only has this happened to me, but there was also this guy I know that happened to sell drugs in the city I moved to. He was always in the club and basically lived there. He ended up getting into a relationship with my homegirls, Nicki. I wasn't very fond of him because I heard about how he treated women, but I didn't say a word. My girl was happy and glowing.

I sometimes like to give people the benefit of the doubt but with a fuckboy that is like believing a venomous snake won't bite you. They moved in together and got engaged real quick. He had already given her a ring, among other "I'm sorry" gifts that she told me about, which she had accepted, and they were working on saving the date. One big problem my friend always complained about was that he was jealous like to the point of being like another woman jealous. Oh my god, we all know how a catty that some men can be.

He was the kind of person that would prefer his girlfriend never to talk to any guy, and it seemed like the only way to make him listen to reason was for her to cut off whoever that person was, even if it was someone close. He was suspect of every male she talked to, if she laughed at a joke on Facebook, whoever it was became one of those he would see as a threat to their relationship regardless of if that was the case or not.

At some point, he insisted that they should share an Instagram. Nicki wasn't cool with it because she already knew how he was and began feeling his vibe and his bad attitude of always being so insecure whenever he saw her talk to any man that was not him. Remember, this is an important characteristic to be cautious of, jealousy. Most men would want other men to think that they have the baddest and have confidence that it wouldn't go any further than just a glance or compliment.

Anyway, he insisted that they had to share their accounts so that there would be no secrets between them and gave her some enchanted happily-ever-after story. After they shared their passwords, he focused on hers. Real street pharmacists don't play around on social media for obvious reasons. If there was a guy that said 'hello" to her in her DMs, he was not having it and shut it down quick. She wasn't allowed to go anywhere without him knowing.

Wherever she was going, he would need the full details about where she was, who she was with, how long she would be there and even would follow up to make sure she was actually there. This was annoying as hell to me, like he didn't have her location on his phone watching her every move anyway. I didn't understand why she stayed at the time and ended up distancing myself because I wanted to do bald-headed hoe things in peace at the time. If we went out, without a shadow of a doubt every time, we had to leave early because here he was blowing her phone up.

At some point, she realized that he was suffocating her. He even tried to go off on one of her siblings online because he thought that he was someone trying to talk to her. It became too much for her to continue putting up with. One thing that made it even more uncomfortable for her was the fact that he was threatened by her success. Nicki was a medical assistant and wanted to go back to school to be a respiratory therapist.

He didn't want her to go far in life. He had a crab mentality and also didn't want her to get ahead of him. Instead of building as a team, he would often tear her down. While most of us were graduating from college, he told her that she shouldn't go to school for anything. This was mainly because he didn't want her to be too close to other guys. When things became too unbearable she finally told him that she was done with him. She thought that they were relationship "goals" until she saw everyone else around her doing better for themselves. When she told him that she wanted to leave, he refused and cried. Nicki stood her ground that she was done. When he saw that she was already used to him crying and wasn't falling for it, he resorted to using suicidal tendencies as an escape route. He would tell her that if she left him, he would commit suicide and she fell for it every time.

It made her feel bad because she grew up in a dysfunctional family environment and knew that he did as well. They had grown close and he was now the only thing she knew as family since he isolated her. She didn't want to leave him because she stopped loving him, but was tired of his fuckboy nature. She just wanted her peace and her freedom. He was one of the most dangerous soul ties out there because he treated her well. Yet, her mental health was declining. The more she stayed with him, the more she felt suffocated.

She denied herself a lot of opportunities; she couldn't even have good friends because of him; her life was just restricted to revolving around him. He used to threaten to commit suicide just to suck her back into feeling sorry for him. At this point, she was uncertain if she wanted to go through with marrying someone like him and postponed the marriage twice.

Nicki ended up getting pregnant by him and wouldn't dare get an abortion because she was against it but knew that having his child would tie her to him for good. In the end, she did leave him after he had held onto her, in the palm of his hand, for four agonizing years. Years that she could never get back. He made her feel guilty over and over again whenever she wanted to leave him by saying she was taking his child away. He made a lot of promises that he was going to change but instead became worse than what he used to be.

He played on her fear but never changed. I was glad when she finally got the courage to leave and when she finally did leave. Guess what? That fool did not die and moved on to ruin the next one's life. She now has a baby to think about raising because of this nigga, but it was worth her having her sanity.

One thing that Nicki never disclosed to me until we reconnected later was how he always tried to gaslight her into thinking that EVERYTHING was her fault. Gaslighting is how people manipulate you into thinking that you are the problem, which isn't the case. If she looked a certain way that wasn't cool with him, didn't cook the eggs right, or just in general, he would put his hands on her, but she thought that it was love. So many of us choose to stay in a relationship because we think the good days outweigh the bad, even in situations like this. Physical abuse is never love.

He had always been the type of dude that would empty his pockets to get the best gift for the woman in his life. He was also the type of dude that would support her financially in regards to shopping, getting her hair and nails done, or whatever she wanted to do and pay all of the bills. He never denied her Cashapp requests or handed her money if he had it with him, and he was in no way broke.

He got expensive gifts for her and who doesn't enjoy those? He also enjoyed spending on her, but once he got mad, he would end up destroying whatever she bought even things that she purchased for the baby. This continued for a long time, and she continued to endure until it got to a point where he beat her up so badly that she ended up in an ICU for a few days. I was a nurse by then, working at the very ICU that she was admitted to, and even was her nurse one night. Nicki made an excuse that her injuries were caused by falling in the shower, but I knew better. I could see the pain and anguish on her face while I was dressing her wounds and it did something to me.

Shortly after, another girl he was involved with found her and decided to send her a message. The girl told her about how he had done the same thing to her recently. Nicki started hearing more about him from those that knew him. Even his own family knew how he was and that he had the same issue with several other women he had talked to previously, but never warned her. No matter how well they treat you. They have no obligation to you by blood. Before then, he had always told Nicki that his ex-girlfriends tried to fight him all the time. She never knew the truth until she ended up lying in a hospital bed.

After a few days, she got discharged from the hospital and decided to leave for her child's sake. Although she wasn't ready to have to face people gossiping about her having a marriage fail. She also didn't want her child to grow up in a broken home that he had created by staying. When she dumped him, she, of course, found someone better who kissed the ground that she and her child walked on. Later on, of course, he came to interrupt her peace and tried to use the age-old baby daddy line, "I want my family back." He tried everything to get her back into his life even after everything he put her through.

What she didn't know is that he had dated several other women after that. He was faithful to them and never cheated on them, but they all dumped him because of his anger issues and how he couldn't control his jealousy. Karma came back to bite him in the ass. Wherever he goes, he always says that women ain't shit if given the opportunity to talk about relationships.

Nicki is now happily married. He isn't in the picture anymore and I see him from time to time and listen to how he complains about all of the women in his life at every function and brings up stories about how Nicki treated him so badly or how she wound up doing his dog ass wrong. The same old sad story. People who weren't there that don't know the whole story believe him. He will tell anyone that cares to listen, but til this day, he fails to realize that he should be a patient at a mental facility. Every time we invite him somewhere, he has a new girlfriend. They usually lose interest in being with him because he continues to be the same phony ass nigga.

Everyone has their breaking point. A breaking point is the point in which, once you get there you stop enduring pain or stop being patient and putting up with a particular situation that you have dealt with for a long time. No matter how much someone is madly in love with you when you reach your breaking point, there's absolutely nothing that can change your mind about moving forward. Everyone deserves to be loved properly.

He continued abusing these women until they got to their breaking point. It didn't matter whether he was handsome, had good dick, and paid all the bills; that's not the only thing needed to make a relationship work. There are other important things needed in a relationship. One big problem some men have is that they fail to realize that just as they want to be respected, women need to be respected too. If you are a good woman but he doesn't respect you, eventually, he will end up losing you and looking dumb just like the rest.

Although the bad boys may have the looks and notoriety, there's nothing wrong with an average guy. These are the men who we tend to friend zone. The ones who would do anything for you, but get taken for granted until it is too late. Ari and Moneybagg Yo are depicted as the ideal couple that glorifies having money, cars, drugs, expensive surgeries, and things that are glorified on TV. But guess what they broke up and her nice car got repo'd. Although despite us all looking for a normal relationship, women and men both aspire to have this type of relationship for some reason. Some call it goals. I call it toxic. If you can't be who you truly are around a person then what is the point? The one who gets friend-zoned will accept you with a bonnet on and an old robe, but here we go chasing ol Moneybagg and end up looking like an idiot.

Everywhere in the world, powerful women or women whom we see as role models get fucked over by men whom they have given their hearts to. I have come to realize that everyone is not built the same. Just as everyone is different, so are their instincts. Some people break down and get back up immediately, while others break down and struggle for the longest to get back up.

The life of a celebrity is something that we sometimes obsess over. Even Lil Durk and India have their problems and recently separated, Dreka and

Kevin Gates did as well. It looks like their life is perfect in public for everyone to see, but in most cases, we don't get to hear about the real things that are happening in their private lives. Yes, we may hear the tabloid stories on TMZ or the Shade Room about how this person cheated or something along those lines. We can speculate but will never know the full story because we weren't there when it all took place. In reality, there are certain types of lifestyles that aren't for everyone. Some people can't wrap their brains around this and choose to be all up in everyone else's business like a Karen. That's why I just mind my own business.

|8|
THE PRETTY BOY

The majority of good-looking guys that are womanizers are those who are good-looking and are proud of it. There goes that pride thing again. They are the ones who know they are handsome because they've been gassed up by thots their entire life and have no problem letting you know that they know they are attractive. The first words I think of to describe such men are sassy and chauvinistic, but I'm sure there are plenty more to describe these dirty, dusty walking STIs that will shoot their shot at any and every woman that they meet just because.

They like to spend a lot of time in the mirror because they fetishize their looks more than anything. This is what we like to call a pretty fuckboy, and they usually identify themselves when they begin to hit puberty in high school. They believe they look better than everyone around them even women which is suspect. They usually chase after women with nice asses and very likely will mess with one they feel is beneath their standards to feel better about themselves. One objective that I've seen them have is to find someone else attractive to have little fuckboy children which usually never works out in the long run. I think that it is truly an insane way of thinking that you can get through life on good looks alone, but that's usually the case in today's society.

Pretty boys still have a lot of mental growing to do. Until they are willing to accept growth, even some little boys assumably have a higher moral code and IQ than them. It's like their state of mind became stagnant once they've figured out they could get over on people with their looks; women can be like this as well. There is a big difference between a little boy and an adult. We were often taught to stay out of grown folks' business and that's exactly what any unsound individual not capable of being realistic should be doing. At this stage of intrinsically being a little boy, he has no business being in a relationship. A little boy still has a lot to learn and a long way to go before he is seen as a man. They say experience is the best teacher.

At some point in their fuckboy's life, I'm sure he has someone he loved or really cared about a lot, but of course, that didn't matter. It didn't stop him from raising that body count higher than Bobby or Orlando Brown with his so-called female friends or anybody else for that matter. In high school, I remember my male friends explaining to me that it was a thing to see who could fuck the most girls, but for an adult? Please go to hell and grow up. The men are not the only ones to blame when it comes to being a thot now. Some women want to be with the most handsome or the most popular men and end up giving away their goods just for a little bit of clout.

They allow him to have his way and end up degrading themselves. Granted some of them do it because they want to be with the guy. Again, who wants a fuckboy? Not me. I know plenty of women are hoping that a pretty fuckboy will want just them, but it never happens that way. Eventually, they find out for themselves that he is not someone that they can have;

they find out that he is community dick. Who will remain community dick until they are washed up, and the dick doesn't even work anymore and that's when they want to settle down. I don't think any woman would take them seriously at this point. He is a one-of-a-kind fuckboy who has a problem like the others and keeps blaming everyone else for it instead of seeing the actual problem.

Have you heard of revenge sex? Revenge sex is primarily thought of as a way to get back at an ex who happened to have done you dirty. It's like the classic eye for an eye bit. After finding out that your crush or someone you were with has been cheating on you, of course, we get mad and want to get back at them. That's when you go on a revenge mission and decide to have sex with someone he knows, someone that if he found out you slept with, would hurt them just as much as what they did to you. And of course, the only option is to do it in a way that he would eventually find out about; but after doing it, then what? It quite possibly won't hurt them at all and end up making you look bad, like a hoe, after the fact.

Perhaps you didn't intend for things to get to that point, but let me tell you, I know all too well that hurt people, hurt people. Certain things can mess with your mental health so bad that sometimes we fail to realize how bitter we have become. Some people choose to be bitter based on their experiences in previous relationships and find this way of thinking or living completely normal.

Everybody has the right to decide what they want for themselves, and people have the right to choose what kind of life they want to live too. It doesn't matter what others feel you should or shouldn't be doing. Blueface and Chrisean Rocks' relationship comes to mind when I think of this. People will always have their own opinion about what path they believe that you need to take, but in the end, everything boils down to what you, in particular, want for yourself.

We are taught this at a young age despite being persuaded by every individual that we come into contact with to do something else. Be that religion, don't eat that or don't do this because it will make you look bad. Ultimately, this decision is yours alone to make once you are an adult. Someone makes the choice to wake up every single day and be a fuckboy.

For example, wild animals often enjoy attacking another animal that either has strength equal to it or it is stronger than. This is because when one animal attacks another if they are somewhat evenly matched, it can put up some sort of fight. In rare instances, the attacker might end up being the one attacked, but in most cases, they have carefully picked out the one they are most interested in pursuing.

Typically in the wild, it has always been such that the stronger animals prey on the weaker animals or the ones that they assume are. They devour them and use them as a means of surviving. Humans are not wild animals but sometimes act as such. Even during periods of scarcity of food, when wild animals of the same species find it difficult to find food to eat, they'll find animals that appear weaker, even if that means turning on animals of their own kind.

All of these things they do for survival. Looking at the survival instincts in plants and wild animals, we would think that it would be different in humans since humans are presumed to be intelligent and evolved, but this is not quite the case. We tend to be somewhat different from wild animals but not completely. Most humans protect their young and don't want them being thrown to the wolves in a sense. Instead of protecting those humans that appear to be weak, some people take advantage of them and, just like those wild animals, prey on them because they can.

Another example is when you watch how plants grow, you notice something interesting about them. First of all, let me just point out that most of us can't keep a plant alive to save our own. I've never had a green thumb and if you do, kudos to you. The majority of the problem may be that too many plants are trying to grow in a small space, like a tiny pot or a studio apartment with no sunlight. They can't get the things that they need to thrive; you see that they begin struggling for nutrients, water, air, and will eventually begin to struggle for space if they so happen to grow in the first place.

The life of plants in this space is all about competition and putting up a fight to survive. Each plant has to fight to outdo the other because they know that they need the essential things for their survival. Among these plants that are struggling for air, water, space, and every available nutrient, there are some that are strong and there are some that are weak, just like people.

These are the plants that will end up losing the battle. One day they're healthy then boom, brown as ever. These are the ones that, if you breathe wrong, they die on you. Charles Darwin propounded a law where he viewed life as the survival of the fittest. I believe he came to bring about this law after watching what was happening around him. The strong ones adapt and become fit, which is a perfect description of the plant that we hate the most, weeds. Weeds can be viewed as fuckboys. They will ruin a beautiful garden to gain the nutrients that they desire.

The stronger living organisms are expected to be the better ones, while the weaker animals are often disregarded. The same goes for us as humans. According to Charles Darwin, the "unfit" may end up not surviving or being at the bottom of the food chain. Enough of my National Geographic rant, fast forward to this day and age or back to reality. What makes someone weaker than another? People tend to judge others quickly from the time that we are children and predominantly will judge us our whole lives.

Being weak doesn't necessarily mean that you are physically weak it could be a social trait like having an unattractive feature that others have deemed as one that people don't desire. These include things that we may or may not help like being born poor, being considered overweight, or just plain ol' ugly. No one wants to be viewed as these things, but it usually ends up happening based on things that are out of our control growing up and can be mentally debilitating. This is why people go to great lengths to change themselves.

I've encountered a lot of people who say that they wish their parents would have done a better job. There is no such thing as a perfect parent or at least not that I know of. Their job is to raise us into adults and that's about it. Some parents are better at this than others. They provide basic necessities we need to grow like plants and protect us from harm. We grow into adults who can decide to take what we have learned and adapt or change what we don't like about ourselves or choose not to.

The adults that we grew up around are the ones who plant the seeds of knowledge that we obtain and help water our brains. Some parents are unfortunately unable to do that. Maybe they were raised in a chaotic environment and didn't adapt. This is where people begin to develop issues involving anger, negative self-image, or other forms of insecurities. And when unresolved, it begins to project those issues on others and they begin bullying or finessing people just to make themselves feel better and begin to adapt in a negative way.

The notion that stronger or more attractive humans are meant to protect the weaker ones has begun to become an outdated one. In most cases, whenever you see an association or a relationship where a stronger human takes on the role of a protector over someone else, looking at this relationship or connection closely, you will find out that the weaker of the two is being exploited. Pretty boys tend to attach to those that seem easier to manipulate as do all fuckboys.

Often women have been known to be the victim or weaker species. This is what people associate you with if you rely on them. Charles Darwin was right, after all, and life is all about the survival of the fittest. Women have now learned how to be strong independently. Instead of being seen as the weaker vessel, we are now matching up with any and everyone that has been portraying themselves as superior.

We have thrown away our submission. Look at Lizzo and others like her living their best life. We have also done away with our docile nature, but who can blame us for this? Women used to be simple people who wanted nothing other than to be treated right by the people we love. We wanted people that would respect us and treat us as equal humans, that would value us and treat us as if we were worth something, but all that we got was the opposite of that and even still do now.

Wise people accept growth as a way of living life. Some experts say that it takes on average 21 days to form a new habit and 66 days to break an old one. The moment people stop growing, they tend to become dead inside while viewing others' thoughts, feelings, and opinions as worthless to them. Even when you have stopped growing physically, you should be growing mentally. We are never too old to learn something new.

Most children get to a point in life where they begin to find that playing with toys seems boring. At what point is this milestone reached? This is when they begin to explore more mature ideas and can comprehend more complex things. At this point, we can assume that they have started growing and begin to form the true personality that they will carry on into adulthood.

Some kids are most known for being bad as hell every day all day, destroying everything they came in contact with, but that doesn't always mean that they will grow into destructive adults. The astounding thing about growing up is being able to be inquisitive and find out things for ourselves with help of course, if lucky. Children tend to find different ways to figure out the world every day. This is why they want to touch or taste things and ask a million and one questions. This is because life is in fact, an ever-changing learning process.

So what about fuckboys you may ask? I'm not saying that they are barbaric cavemen impervious to the ability to change. If they decide to remain fuckboys, that just shows they enjoy the toxic way of thinking. And will only be remembered as the man that tears women down, breaks up the family dynamic, and enjoys bringing women to tears for their own enjoyment—the ones who care about him. Then call themselves getting mad or wanting pity when life hasn't turned out the way that they expected or they lost the realest one on their team by continuing to play games. Karma will eat their asses alive. When it's as simple as stopping instead, they'd rather look like a fool by refusing to grow up and change.

Granted there are many issues that could lead someone to feel the need to be a fuck boy. We discussed some of these in the beginning, and I know that there are a million and one reasons. But when someone is caught committing a crime, they usually won't admit it until they are caught. We all hate to be called out on our BS, but this is how we get wiser and learn from our mistakes.

Remember when the Coronavirus pandemic first hit? It was some scary shit. The whole world was a stand-still had to shut down because everyone was terrified and had no clue about what was going on. A lot of people were laid off or even lost their jobs. As a result of the mass loss of jobs, there was an increase in the rate of crime. Some people committed crimes as a means to be able to provide for themselves and their families. Does that make it right? Absolutely not. They could've found a better way, but they made the choice not to. So when they got caught, indeed, they weren't exempt from the law, but if they didn't get caught, I'm sure they ain't saying a word about it.

Like with the business PPP loan, a lot of people got one knowing damn well they were not running a business, but the government wasn't checking, so it was basically free money. We all wanted to get one after that. Hell, I know that I did, but dealing with the consequences of getting caught deferred many of us from doing so. Even though politicians, billionaires, and a ton of people do this type of thing on a daily basis that doesn't make it right.

They aren't held accountable for their actions just like a fuckboy; If everybody going through a hard time had to steal because of how difficult things are for them, who would be the ones getting screwed over? My point here is this, whether or not you think your actions are not affecting someone, chances are they ARE. The reason dating has become such a treacherous experience now is because everyone has become a fuckboy in a sense. Everyone only cares about themselves which is innate, but at what cost? The next generation will likely suffer because of this and everyone will grow accustomed to fuckboys being the new norm if we haven't already.

Why is this so? Because we have too many fuckboys around that we aren't calling out. We have fuckboys as our siblings, and we have fuckboys that act as parents, we have fuckboys that act as uncles, we have fuckboys that act as friends, we have fuckboys that act as husbands, we have fuckboys that act as bosses; we have fuckboys everywhere. When people think that you are weak and rely on them for protection, the majority will take advantage of it and use it as means to gain something for themselves.

|9|
ACCOUNTABILITY

Okay, one other question that I would like to ask ya'll, and I promise this is the last one is, to what extent would you go to cover up something that you did and didn't want anyone else to find out? This doesn't necessarily include cheating or stealing. We have all done one or even multiple things that we are most certainly not proud of. When do you get to the point in life where you say fuck it? This is me. This is what I've done. Either accept it or don't and decide not to let that thing define you or turn you into this evil supervillain. This, my beautiful friend, is called accountability.

There are so many people out there that went through hell in their life when they were younger, but they grew up to become better people. There are also people that grew up watching the ones they loved being abused. It affected them to the point that they vowed never to treat any other individual this way. They tell themselves that under no circumstance will they ever allow themselves to treat the woman they love or any woman that way. Well, I can tell you that may or may not be the case. All situations have different circumstances, but choosing to mistreat another person is always a choice. Why do that when you could just easily listen to your conscience instead of blocking it out and walk away?

I haven't met too many men that hold their homeboys accountable for their actions but, I have met some so it's not an impossible notion. On one hand, you have this amazing man who treats women right, but you will look at who he hangs around, and there is Sneaky Stevie over there in the cut being an asshole and treating every female that he encounters like shit. Do men police their friends like women sometimes do? More often than not whenever we see someone wearing something ugly we will say "your friends are not your friends because they would've told you not to wear that outfit." I have noticed that females tend to be more sound in judgment and correct their friends if they feel they are doing wrong. Let me rephrase that; GOOD friends will let you know that you are fucking up in a way that is not malicious but rather to help you out because they love you. And if they don't, my advice is that you need to find better friends.

Most men have homeboys that they grew up with in the same type of environment. Yet, different households harness different results. Even some siblings in the same household who were raised exactly the same by the same parents can yield different types of individuals with different personalities. We can't choose our families, but we can choose our friends and often influence the choices that they make. So with this being the case, why not hold them accountable for their actions if you care?

This brings me to an interesting point. Most women are taught the value and meaning of love and self-worth by the male figures that they grew up around. You would think that it would only be right for men to police each other for the sake of their mothers, sisters, daughters, aunts, friends, and even female cousins. Yet, for years, women have continued to be exploited. We relied heavily on men for protection, but somewhere along the lines, things changed and instead of protecting us, they turned against us and began calling us difficult. We are at a crossroads. Right now, we don't want anyone protecting us and have now learned to protect ourselves and our own peace. Because if you don't protect yourself, no one else will. Even though we get on each other's last nerve, it is still agreed that men and women do need each other though.

But the "City Girls" and other celebrities are now becoming the images that young women growing up are seeing and trying to emulate because society has made it this way. The idea of being "FNF(Fuck Nigga Free)" has become a term that is seen in a negative light, but I beg to differ. Women in other cultures still find themselves being held to the standard practice of being submissive. Their environment, to some extent, involves upholding the old ways, but even these women have to deal with surviving encounters with fuckboys. We all have gotten a taste of the carnage that they cause and now are striving to be like Lori Harvey, who already knew what these niggas were capable of.

Here's the thing, there's a difference between living for yourself and taking control of your life or just trying to live off of someone else. If you choose to be some type of aristocratic socialite and enjoy the spotlight or material things, then that's your business. I don't believe in leading people on. In fact, it is one of my pet peeves and a pretty terrible thing to do to someone in my opinion.

These 'city girls' have already started protecting themselves and their hearts. They are done looking at men to protect them, and they will never allow any man to take advantage of them again and most definitely live freely. They already learned that the world is a tough place, and nobody will protect you better than you can protect yourself. Fuckboys pretend to offer you protection, but once you lower your guard, they exploit and do whatever you allow them to. Nobody wants to go through this same unpleasant story over and over again.

Once feelings are involved, we grow accustomed to dealing with someone and tend to form expectations of them. Now, some people form unrealistic expectations that may be due to underlying reasons or personal issues that we may never know about that they need to address, but for the most part; you can control who you interact with enough to the point that you will know if you are interested in continuing to pursue more with them or not because they meet them. If expectations are set low, that is who you will attract. Low-grade men. Like SZA said in her song "Broken Clocks," that she loved dirty men since she was 10. I am guilty of this same thing. Sometimes we overlook the facts because we want to be with that person so bad, but they don't feel the same and thus get friend-zoned or end up friend zoning somebody that could be the right person for us. Don't miss your blessing.

I have come to believe that we meet different people in our lives for different reasons. From my own personal experience, I have come to agree totally with this. There are people I met in my life that helped shape it, good or bad. But despite that, all of these people added a lot of value to my life. I don't know what life would be like if I didn't meet these people because then I wouldn't have learned to grow and adapt.

Sometimes I reminisce about the simple incidents that brought these people into my life and come to the realization that in most cases it was unplanned. Although I do like to think that everything happens for a reason as if there was a script that had already been written down for us to meet and act out. Call it fate.

When certain people came into my life, I didn't think that anything special would come out of it. I don't think that I knew things would turn out the way that they turned out now but I am grateful for the lessons that I did learn. Some of these people are still in my life, and some of them aren't anymore. And may I just say good riddance. Learning when to let go is one of the most crucial abilities to possess in this day and age. I was talking to a friend of mine over brunch and she gave me the best advice that I have ever received in my life that I would like to share with you.

After falling for these same types of niggas repeatedly, she told me that I should make a list and write down the pros and cons of talking to this particular person. We've all done this before right? She said the only thing I would like for you to do differently is after each pro and each con, write "he doesn't want me" after each one. I was floored. It was the simplest concept yet so effective. It's often hard telling ourselves the truth but a necessary evil. You have to place value on yourself. How are you gone win when you ain't right within?

Whether those people are still in my life or not, one thing is certain: they impacted my life and directed my path to become a better person. I have learned to become my own source of happiness. And also that you can't take accountability of how someone else views you. I am not the only woman with this story. Some, not all, women in the world have similar stories, and they have people that they met that affected their life in some shape, form, or fashion. Some of these people made positive impacts, while others made negative ones. These different people we met at different seasons opened different chapters in our lives, and some of them brought us a particular kind of laughter or memories that we won't forget. Among all these people we met, the most difficult ones we have been forced to encounter are fuckboys.

One of the few things that still gives hope to some is the idea of love. Being in love, loving somebody, and receiving it back. So many people see love as their means of hope, as their means of finding peace in this world of hardship and sorrow. It's human nature. We put a lot of energy into it, dedicate our time to it, and deserve to be loved properly in return. This is why we put our best into it, but when you do this, you need to be the recipient of genuine love in return.

People tend to use lame excuses of why they do bad things to others because something went wrong earlier in their life. Do you find that reason enough? Do you think that using your past life as an excuse to hurt people who did nothing wrong to you, people who deserve the best from you, is a valid reason? If you still have a conscience, you should know the right answer to this question.

In conclusion, women are always blamed for our choices in men. Despite being tricked and lied to, somehow, it is always our fault that we got the wrong guys that subsequently treated us like garbage. I was in a deadbeat baby mama/baby daddy group on Facebook and the whole premise of the group was to bash black women and say that they need to make better choices in men and keep their legs closed so they won't end up with a deadbeat baby daddy. Who do we blame for this? If not ourselves, then who? If we had made our decisions differently, we imaginably wouldn't have ended up with the fuckboy that we let make a mess out of our life. Everyone makes mistakes.

I consider myself an empath. An empath has the ability to be in tune with others and can feel how they feel, some people more so than others. I can feel how someone is feeling even from miles away through text, phone conversation or in person, yet when your judgment is clouded by a fuckboy you can't always see things clearly. Even after they have clearly shown you who they truly are. We ignore many red flags in the name of love, but now we can use the tools we have gathered throughout life to change that and hold ourselves accountable. So, wipe your tears and dust yourself off sis.

In this book, I have identified a few types of fuckboys, but there are a number of others that I may not have mentioned. Again, I am not saying that all men are the same. There are men that when they come into your life will sweep you off your feet and love you in a way that makes you feel like you have never experienced being loved like this before in your life. These men make you realize that all the other ones from the past weren't real men. They will make you feel as if you are the only woman in the world. They will effortlessly be all about you, not just when you are looking but when you are not too. They make you trust them, even though they may get on your nerves at times but you know that they would never do anything to break that trust that you already built. Loyal men are a dime a dozen. And good men are definitely hard to find.

The good ones don't mind making compromises just to make you happy and just to be with you. The only thing that these men are really after is how to put a smile on your face. They find happiness in seeing you happy. Once these men see you in pain, your pain becomes theirs and they'll do anything to let you know that. Like a best friend, they can feel when you are suffering. They do all they can to make sure they ease any pain that you are battling.

If you need a shoulder to cry on, they will always be there to offer you their shoulder, they will never desert you, and they will never ever use your secrets against you. They will try to protect you from falling into harm's way, and they will never hurt you intentionally. Recently, the term "simp" has been the label given to men who are attentive to their women, and most don't want to be clowned by their homeboys for doing it. Although these men do exist one thing I found out over the years is that we women end up not being attracted to them. We end up not falling for them. We find it so easy to fall for fuckboys because they have more to show off and know how to attract us to them.

Whenever a fisherman wants to fish with a hook, he always has something that serves as bait which he attaches to the hook before letting it down into the water. The bait is meant to attract the fish to the hook. Normally when you put down a hook without bait or something intriguing on it, the majority of fish would be dense enough to go closer to it or even give it a second thought. If you don't stand true to yourself and define what you really want, you might end up taking the bait. Hook, line, and sink her.

Life is all about risks, and some people know that what they are planning to venture into has a lot of risks attached to it, but they still go for it because they know that there is a chance at being successful, which is something that a great deal of us strive for. There is hardly anything that can bring success in life that doesn't have any risks attached to it. Starting a business, for example, has a lot of risks attached. When someone decides to get into any kind of business, this person should already know some of the risks. If things end up working out fine, this person will enjoy his or her success, but businesses also fail sometimes due to unforeseen circumstances.

Despite all of the scary things that can happen in life, we still take risks. We are all here for a purpose, and I'm not saying don't date a fuckboy because you may just be the person that the universe sent to change them, and who knows, may end up in a fairytale but don't put all of your eggs in one basket. The reward that comes with true love isn't impossible. This is why despite the risks involved, we still continue to involve ourselves with fuckboys.

We have to remember that no man or woman is one hundred percent perfect. You can build up with a man, but remember, they may not be right for you and have their own mind. Most men that seem to be what you envisioned as everything you want end up being fuckboys. You have to be careful so you don't end up being a victim.

Make sure that you don't get deceived by what shows on the surface. Don't be easily moved by what you see superficially or by what you hear, only by actions my dear. Because we all know that they speak louder than words. The pain associated with loving someone can be brutal, and this is more of a reason why we have to guard our hearts and practice self-love to the highest extent; if we love ourselves, we won't intentionally walk into an open trap set by a fuckboy. So many women have found themselves repeatedly asking after being treated like shit, what have I done wrong? What did I do to deserve this? You won't be the first nor the last to treat a man better than you treat yourself and be blindsided by the treatment received in return.

I would like to know what type of fuckboys have you dealt with. Think about it. We all eventually find out that we have been dealing with one when those characteristics rear their ugly faces. The next step would be holding ourselves and each other accountable by doing things differently from past experiences that we have learned from and having realistic expectations of people.

I wish that when I was younger and growing up that I had someone grab me by the hand and say," when someone shows you who they are, believe them the first time." To all young women that have fallen prey like me, we are all searching for our knight in shining armor like Remy found Papoose, Michelle found

Barack Obama, or Russell Wilson, but without Ciara's prayer, we just hope and pray that we don't get involved and end up having fuckboy problems.

9 798986 841700